The Temple of the Blind

Book One

The Box

Brian Harmon

The Box

ISBN: 1463616295

ISBN-13: 978-1463616298

For Guinevere

Chapter 1

It was just a stupid wooden box.

But it was also a mystery. It was not just that Albert didn't know where it came from or how it found its way into his locked car while he was in class. It was not just the cryptic markings etched into its sides. It was not even that he still didn't know what was inside. It was the *sum* of all of these things. It was the fact that nothing about the box was obvious. It was an enigma literally locked up within itself…and that was *irresistibly* fascinating.

He had been studying it all afternoon. He'd already missed lunch and if he didn't watch the time he'd be eating dinner from a vending machine. He'd thought of little else since returning from his eleven o'clock class, and he didn't even know if there was anything to be learned from it. Yet each time he walked away, he soon found himself back at his desk, staring again at the box.

It was a ten-inch cube with no apparent seam to indicate a lid and no visible hinges. He had turned it over and over in his hands and could not determine how it was supposed to open. Yet there was something inside. Things rattled when he shook it. Also, on one side there was a lock, which indicated that the box did indeed open, but the revolving brass plate made a mystery of which end belonged up. The keyhole was about the size of a nickel, with a narrow slit suggesting that the key was very simple, perhaps just a narrow piece of flat metal, but he was unable to pick the lock with a pocketknife.

With the exception of a few small scars in the wood, there were no distinguishing marks on the keyhole side of the box. On each of the other five sides, however, someone had used a sharp object to carve into the wood. On three of these sides were written strange cryptic messages while the last two displayed something that appeared to be a sort of map.

He leaned back in his chair and tried to focus. He

never before thought of inanimate objects as having personality, but this box did. He felt almost that it *enjoyed* being mysterious, that it mocked his ignorance. It was like a deeply intriguing character in a really good mystery novel. But in a mystery novel, the secrets are always eventually revealed. Whatever secrets this box held might never be relinquished, might not even exist, as far as he knew. And that made the mystery all the more exquisite.

Derek, Albert's roommate, entered the room and dropped his keys onto his desk. "You still staring at that thing?"

Albert glanced at the clock. It was already almost five. "Yep."

"I think you're making way too much out of this. Somebody probably got the wrong car or something."

Albert did not respond. It was a possibility he'd more than considered. After all, it was only early September, just a couple short weeks into his first semester here at Briar Hills University. Having come from as far north as St. Louis, he knew no one and hadn't made more than a handful of acquaintances, none of whom knew him well enough to distinguish his car from all the others that occupied the parking lot the previous evening. Whoever left the box could very well have meant to leave it in someone else's car.

"I wouldn't stress about it."

Albert did not turn around. He could hear the familiar tones as Derek checked his cell phone for voicemail. He'd only been living with Derek Clarnet for three and a half weeks, but he already knew his every routine by heart. Every time he returned from class he would walk straight to his desk and drop his keys and wallet. Then he would always reach for his cell phone and check his voicemail. He never took it with him to class for some reason. If there were any messages that required a response, he would do so. And he would always play Solitaire while he talked on the phone. Every time, as soon as he was finished dialing, he would sit down at his computer and load the game. The moment he hung up, he would turn it off. It didn't matter whether he was losing or winning. Once he was done with that he would pocket the phone and leave through the bathroom to visit with Scott and David, their suitemates in the next room. He would return after a while for his keys and wallet and then disappear until later that evening, anywhere between eight and eleven, depending on how much homework awaited him. He would then sit at his desk and work until exactly midnight, when he would go straight to bed. He rose every morning at a quarter to seven and showered and shaved. He left for his first class right at seven thirty. He always ate lunch at eleven. He always ate dinner at half past four. He was, without a doubt, the most boring human being Albert had ever met in his life, and he was actually surprised at how annoying that was.

"'See Carrie,'" Derek read aloud.

Albert realized that he was reading the Post-It he'd left on his keyboard and sat up. "Oh yeah. Carrie from across the hall. She was looking for you while you were at dinner."

"Did she say what she wanted?"

Albert shook his head. "Nope." *And I didn't care to ask*, he thought. He'd recognized the girl as one of the four who lived in the suite across the hall, but he did not know her name until she asked him if he would tell Derek that "Carrie was looking for him." She was a very pretty brunette, petite, with shy mannerisms and a freckled face.

Derek said nothing more. He returned the phone to his desk and then stepped into the bathroom and locked the door. At six-foot-three, he appeared awkward at first sight. He was scrawny, almost geeky, but with his neat hair and piercing brown eyes, he was still fairly handsome. He was also very charming when he wanted to be. Albert had been sharing this room with him for only a short time, but it was already perfectly clear how they were going to get along. The two of them could coexist peacefully enough; their different interests made this room one of the only places on campus where they were ever likely to cross paths. Albert was a computer science major. Derek was a business major. Albert liked to read; Derek liked to go out. They would never be friends. In fact, Albert could hardly stand the guy. Besides his maddeningly boring routines, he was arrogant, self-centered, stubborn, closed-minded, cold natured and lacked any real sense of humor. Yet he was manipulative. He could suddenly become the most lovable human being alive when he wanted something, a tactic that Albert found dazzlingly obnoxious.

Albert had already noticed the time Derek was spending across the hall, trying his best to turn on the charm for Carrie and her suitemates. The names on their doors were Carrie, Danielle, Gail and Tanya. He was pretty sure that Gail was the heavyset blonde and now he knew which one was Carrie, but he still did not know which of the remaining two was Danielle and which was Tanya.

Derek returned from the bathroom, snatched his keys off the desk and left the room without speaking a word. A moment later his voice drifted back from across the hall.

Albert spent no time wondering about Derek or Carrie. He turned his attention back to the box and immersed himself again in its curious secrets.

He'd questioned everyone he knew about the box. He even called his parents and sister to see if they knew anything about it, half expecting it to be some sort of bizarre, belated birthday present, but no one knew anything about it. Everyone seemed to have the same opinion: that someone left it there by mistake.

He supposed he could just break the box open. He

could smash it or saw through it. It was only wood. But he did not want to damage it until he'd had a chance to find the sender. After all, it might be important to somebody. Besides, he didn't want to destroy any of the markings before he could decipher them.

Each of the box's three messages was written using only straight lines roughly gouged into the wood. This left some characters frustratingly ambiguous. On one side, for example, there were ten characters arranged in three rows. To Albert, they appeared to read,

I Z

V I I

I O O S T

but it was difficult to be certain. It was impossible to tell whether some of these characters represented numbers or letters. The straight vertical lines could have been the number one or the letter I, for example. Or even a lower-case L. The S could have been a five. The two Os in the bottom line were drawn as squares, and could have been zeros instead, or for all he knew they could actually have been intended as squares. There was simply no way to know for sure, which made the clue that much more puzzling.

He had pondered over these three lines for hours now, trying to decipher them. The middle line could have been the Roman numeral seven, but with nothing else to go on, and no idea how to decipher the other two, he had no way of knowing for certain. It could be a V and an eleven. For that matter, the lines comprising the V were slightly crossed at the bottom. It could even have been a sloppy X.

Frustrated, he turned the box around.

Perhaps the most haunting of the messages was written on the side opposite the keyhole. Here there were five lines. The first four were complete words. From top to bottom they read HELP, COME, TOGETHER and YESTERDAY. The fifth line was not a word, but just three letters: G, N and J.

These lines were much easier to read than the previous three, even with their straight-line lettering, but with the legibility came a haunting feeling. Help. Come. It was as though someone were calling out to him for something. But what could yesterday mean? Was it literal? If so, he'd received the box the previous evening, so yesterday would have been two days ago. Or did it mean the past in general? Help come together yesterday. It made no sense. And how did the last line fit in? Perhaps it was someone's or something's initials.

The final side of the box was carved with only seven letters, scrawled across the surface diagonally from corner to corner, in larger letters than the other messages.

B R A N D Y R

He thought that he recognized these letters. It looked like a name. Brandy R. He knew a Brandy R. Or at least he'd *met* a Brandy R. Brandy Rudman was his lab partner in Chemistry. She was a sophomore, one year ahead of him and likewise a year older, nearly twenty, while he was barely nineteen, yet she could have passed as a sixteen-year-old high school student, small and girlish with a soft face and small, modest figure. She was very pretty. He had not expected to find a lab partner so quickly, but she was sitting in front of him on that first day and when the instructor told them to pair off she turned around, scanning the other students in the class until her pretty eyes fell on him. "You mind?" she asked simply, to which he replied a startled "Sure."

It was just dumb luck for him. He'd been attending classes for not yet a day and a half at a school where he recognized no one and instead of being the last lonely student standing around looking for a pair that would allow him to join, as he'd expected to be, he found himself paired off almost at once and with a very pretty young woman. And by even greater luck, she had so far turned out to be a very lovely person to know as well, friendly, kind, outgoing and fun.

His Chemistry lab was scheduled for Tuesdays and Thursdays at ten o'clock in the morning. Today was Thursday. That morning he stuffed the box inside his green backpack and took it with him to class, intending to see if she knew anything about it, but she was as ignorant of its origins as everyone else he'd spoken with, his last chance at an answer severed at its root.

"Must be another Brandy R.," she'd concluded, peering down into his backpack at the strange, wooden box. "I've never seen it before. It was in your car?"

"Yeah. All the doors were still locked. Nothing broken."

"Weird."

Weird was right. It was also disappointing. A part of him had hoped for an excuse to get to know Brandy a little better.

Albert turned and looked at the clock again. It was after five now. He needed to go eat dinner. He usually tried to go before Derek returned. The less time he spent with him the better.

He stood up and stretched. Some time away from the box would do him good. He was becoming frustrated with it again. Perhaps everyone was right, perhaps the box was never meant for him and he would never understand where it came from or what it meant. But that thought became like a looming darkness. He did not want to be left ignorant. He wanted to know about this box. He wanted to understand it. He didn't like to leave mysteries unsolved. It simply wasn't his nature.

He was reaching for his shoes when the phone rang. It would probably be somebody looking for Derek.

Somebody was always looking for Derek. It was funny how Albert was always looking to avoid him.

He sat down on the bed and answered the phone.

"Is Albert there?"

It was a woman's voice, feminine, petite, pretty. "Speaking," he replied.

"Hi. This is Brandy. From Chem."

Albert stood up again, surprised. They exchanged numbers the first day of class in case either of them missed and needed notes, but he never expected her to use it. "Hi."

"Hey, did you find anything out about that box?"

"No. Not a thing." His heart sped up a notch when she told him who she was. Now it jumped again, shifting from second to third.

Brandy was quiet for so long that he began to think the line was disconnected, but before he could ask if she was still there she said, "There was something in my car when I left class today."

Fourth gear. He started walking across the room, pacing as he sometimes did when he was on the phone. "What did you get?"

Instead of answering, she said, "You're in Lumey, right?"

"That's right." Lumey Hall was the most expensive dormitory on campus. He'd spent the extra money for the semi-private bathroom and coed environment. From his first tour of the Hill he did not like the prison-like feel of the community halls elsewhere on campus, so he forked over nearly twice what other freshmen were paying in the Cube. Over here, two rooms made up a suite and a bathroom connected the two, so only four people shared facilities, instead of an entire floor. Also, unlike any other building, Lumey was entirely coed, hence the fact that there were girls living right across the hall from him. And since Lumey was usually reserved for students with a junior standing or higher, he was very fortunate to obtain his room. It turned out that the freshmen dormitories were overcrowded. In the next few years they would probably have to build a new one.

"What floor?"

"Second floor. Room two-fourteen."

"Meet me in the second floor lounge. I'll be there in about twenty minutes."

"Okay."

She hung up without saying goodbye and he stood staring at the dead phone, his mind a cyclone of thoughts. He was about to get information about the box. Maybe together they would figure out what it was and who gave it to him.

Chapter 2

Twenty minutes turned out to be twenty-five. Albert would be the first to agree that five minutes was hardly an eternity, but Brandy knew something about the box, something she was not willing to disclose over the phone. Now every minute passed like an hour as he sat in the second floor lounge of Lumey Hall, waiting to see what she knew.

There was something in my car when I left class today. Those words kept ringing in his ear. He remembered how he'd unlocked his car the previous evening and found the box sitting in the driver's seat. It was a frightening experience. He did not even see it until he opened the door. Brandy at least found her package in broad daylight, but it still must have been unnerving, perhaps even more so since whoever left it there was bold enough to get into her car in the middle of a busy school day.

The box had Brandy's name on it. Now Brandy had found something too, and in exactly the same way, no less. Perhaps it was no accident after all that he found himself in possession of the box.

At the other end of the room, two boys were playing table tennis. One was a skinny blond kid, his face a spattering of pimples. The other was of an average build with a red goatee that wasn't quite thick enough yet to completely cover his chin. Nearby, a skinny girl with raven black hair cut short enough to stand on end sat in one of the plush chairs watching them. She was close enough to them in such an empty room to indicate that she was with them, but her eyes kept drifting from the boys to the door to her watch and back again, suggesting that she, too, was waiting for someone.

The steady *plink-plunk* sound of the ping-pong ball could be annoying at times, but tonight Albert found it and the occasional outbursts of frustration and excitement from the boys relaxing, almost hypnotic. It was a perfect distraction for his senses. Too much silence made him think too much and just lately that made his head hurt.

He was sitting off to one side of the room, positioned so that he could see out of the lounge and down the hallway to the main doors. Lumey was built on the slope of a hill, so on the back side of the building the first floor was the ground floor, but on the front—the side he was facing now—the main doors led in on the second floor. The visitor parking lot and the meters were located on this side of the building. Therefore, he'd determined that this was the direction from which Brandy would most likely enter.

He spotted her as she was climbing the steps. She was wearing a dark shirt and jeans, different from the shorts and tank top she'd been wearing that morning in lab. She was clenching a black leather purse in her left hand and carried a cigarette in her right.

Albert thought that there was something stiff about her. She looked tense. He watched her as she paused at the ashtray outside the door. She drew one last time from the cigarette and then crushed it. As she did so, she turned and looked around, as though she expected someone to be watching her.

Of course there *was* someone watching her, but he didn't think that it was him she was looking around for.

Perhaps he was imagining it. Maybe she heard something somewhere, someone yelling or a car horn blaring. Maybe he was simply looking for things that weren't there. Puzzling over the box for so many hours had caused his imagination to run a little wild.

At last she opened the door and walked in. Almost immediately, her eyes found him. Albert stood up and greeted her and immediately the smell of her cigarette tickled his nose. He was not a smoker and did not like the smell of cigarettes, but his mother smoked and he was used to it enough that he was not really bothered by it. He always said it would have to be a pretty fine line between yes and no to turn down a date based on whether a girl smoked.

"Sorry I'm late," she said as she sat down.

"It's okay."

She did not relax at first. She held her purse in her lap and looked at him. Albert realized right away that there was something cold about her, as though he had done her some grave evil of which he was not yet aware. Her eyes were a soft and gorgeous shade of blue behind the gold-rimmed lenses of her small glasses, beautiful enough to be hypnotizing, but when she leaned forward they were focused so fiercely on him that it made him want to shrink away. "I'm just going to say right now that if this is some kind of practical joke I'm not going to be happy. There are laws against breaking into someone's car, you know."

Albert stared at her, his own dark eyes wide and shocked. Those words struck him like a hammer. He'd never even considered a practical joke. That cast a whole new light on the subject. What if someone was trying to pull something on him? What if someone somewhere was laughing his ass off at his silly obsession with that nonsense box? "If it's a practical joke," he said, almost numb with the realization of that possibility, "then we're two cheeks on the same butt of it."

Brandy watched his expression as he spoke, her eyes stony and piercing. Finally, after a moment, she laughed. It was a quick sound, a huff of air, almost a sigh. In an instant her features melted back into that sweet, ladylike girlishness that he'd seen so often in the classroom. She relaxed back into her chair, her posture slightly slouched, comfortable. She gazed at him through her glasses, her eyes once more soft and sweet. Her hair was very light blonde, a little past shoulder-length, straight and smooth with short bangs. She was wearing a simple, short-sleeved shirt, black with red patterns around the neck and sleeves. Albert couldn't stop himself from noticing the low neckline. She was not big-breasted, but neither was she shapeless. She was quite pretty, blessed with a girlish figure and a soft and delicate complexion.

Overall, she was a sharp contrast to him. Whereas her hair and eyes were light and fair, his were dark and deep. Her nose and chin were soft and round, while his were straight and pronounced, almost pointed. He was rather short, although still a couple inches taller than she, and a little stocky, and he appeared bulky compared to the soft curves of her petite figure.

"I'm sorry," said Brandy. "I don't mean to accuse you of anything. I wasn't trying to be a bitch."

"No, don't worry about it."

"It's just kind of scary, you know. Somebody got into my car while I was in class."

"I understand. I mean this is some pretty weird stuff."

"I almost threw it away. I didn't want it, really. It kind of gave me the creeps."

These words were like a slap in the face. She almost threw it away? "What did you get?"

She opened her purse and withdrew a small brown pouch. "I feel silly even bringing this to you, but I guess it sort of belongs to you." She opened the pouch, which appeared to be made of soft, aged leather, pulled closed with a simple piece of coarse twine, and then emptied it into her left hand. She turned her eyes up to his as she held it out to him. "It's a key."

Albert stared at it for a moment before taking it from her. It was a flat piece of brass with a simple ring for a grip and a single tooth on each side. Just looking at it, he could understand why he was unable to pick the lock with the pocketknife. Even though the key was flat instead of round or grooved, it still required teeth to work the tumblers inside the lock.

He reached out and took it from her warm palm. He felt a million miles away, as though he were staring at it through a television set instead of holding it in his own fingers. It didn't feel real. He turned it over, almost mesmerized, and suddenly he was drawn back with a slap. Seven letters were scratched onto this side of the key, just like on one side of the box. But instead of B R A N D Y R, the key read A L B E R T C.

"Albert Cross?" Brandy guessed.

"Seeing as how you're the only Brandy R. I know and I'm probably the only Albert C. you know," he replied, "I'd say it's a pretty good bet."

"Do you think whoever gave us these things got them mixed up? Mine had your name and yours had mine?"

Albert shook his head. "But then we wouldn't know where to find the other half."

"Yeah. That's true." Brandy's eyes dropped to the backpack at Albert's feet. "Did you bring the box?"

"Yeah."

"Can I see it?"

"Of course." Albert unzipped the bag, removed the

box and handed it to her. "After my American History class last night I walked out to my car and it was just waiting for me. I'm in there from six to nine. It was in the driver's seat. I always lock my doors."

Brandy held the box in her lap as she studied it. "My car was in the commuter lot next to Wuhr." The Daniel R. Wuhr Building was the science and math building on campus. It was where their Chemistry classrooms were located. "It was right there in my driver's seat after class today."

"Did you have your doors locked?"

Brandy shrugged, almost embarrassed. "They were locked when I came back out, but I have a bad habit of not locking my doors. Whoever put the bag there could've locked them."

Albert nodded. "I can't be a hundred percent sure of mine, either, actually. I say I always lock them, but every now and then..."

Brandy stared at the box as she held it in her lap, her eyes fixed on the letters of her name. "I didn't say anything earlier, but when you showed this to me the first time there was just something eerie about it. It gave me chills. I didn't even want to touch it." She turned it over in her hands, looking at each side. "I'm not sure I want to be holding it now."

Albert said nothing. He watched her expression for a moment and then followed her gaze to the box.

"Brandy R.," she read.

"Yeah. I guess we know for sure what that side means now."

"You haven't figured any of the other sides out?"

"Nope. Maybe they'll make sense once we open it." Albert looked down at the key he was holding. He could feel a cold tingle of excitement rising up his spine.

"Maybe." Brandy turned the box again, observing the other sides. "Well these are all Beatles songs."

Albert's eyes snapped from the key to the box. "What?"

"'Help', 'Come Together' and 'Yesterday' are all songs by the Beatles."

Albert stared at the words on the side of the box. "Are you sure?"

"Of course I'm sure." She glanced up at him, met his eyes for just a brief moment, then looked back down, as if she detected the hungry attention her revelation had drawn from him and was disturbed by it. "I like music. I listen to a lot of it. All different kinds. I don't know what 'G N J' means, though."

Albert felt numb. "The Beatles." He might have recognized country or pop titles, but The Beatles?

"That doesn't mean that's what these mean," Brandy explained. "It could just be a coincidence. But they *are* Beatles songs."

"Wow. I'm impressed."

Brandy looked up at him again. This time she smiled a little.

"Any clue about the other side?"

Brandy turned the box again and tried to read it. "Just looks like garbage to me."

Albert nodded. "Yeah. Me too."

"But these last two sides are a map, right?"

Albert nodded. "Yeah, but I don't know what it's a map of."

"Maybe it's inside."

"Maybe." He looked down at the key again. "Let's see."

Brandy looked up at him, but made no move to hand him the box. "Do you think we should?"

"What do you mean?"

Brandy shrugged. She looked extremely uncomfortable. "I'm just not sure about this. Somebody went to a lot of trouble to set this all up. Why?"

Albert stared back at her, unable to answer.

"I mean this thing still gives me the creeps. It's just too weird. It's like something out of a... I don't know. An Alfred Hitchcock movie or... Or a Stephen King short story. It's just not *natural*, you know."

Albert looked down at the box. She was right. It was *very* unnatural. Inside, he'd understood that all along.

"I don't want to sound crazy, but there's a part of me that really thinks that maybe we should just throw it away. Forget about it."

This suggestion hit Albert like a punch in the gut. How could he just forget about it? That box had commanded his every thought since he first laid eyes on it. But then again, wasn't that reason enough to do just as she suggested? Perhaps she was right. Perhaps it *was* unhealthy, even dangerous.

The two of them sat there, each of them staring at the box.

"There's also a part of me," Brandy added, a little cautiously, "that still doesn't trust you."

Albert looked up at her, surprised.

"I mean I don't know anything about this. One day, out of the blue, you show up to class with this box with my name on it and say you found it in your car. After class I go to *my* car and find a key with your name on it. And I really don't know you."

Albert lowered his eyes all the way to the floor. She certainly made a point. "That's true." He nodded and looked back up at her. "I guess I really can't expect you to trust me. I really don't have reason to trust *you*."

Brandy started to say something, but she stopped herself.

"As far as I know, *you* could've left that box in my car. After all, I have no way of knowing whether you're telling me the truth about how you came by this key. For the same reason, you have no way of knowing how I came by that box or that I didn't put the key in your car."

"Yesterday you beat me to class and I left before you

did…"

Albert was impressed. She'd really thought this through. "But I could've had an accomplice."

"Yeah."

He leaned back against the cushions of the couch and stared down at the key. Three more people had entered the room since Brandy arrived. Two were young men who were speaking a language he could not place and playing a game of chess. The third was a young woman with a huge mane of curly black hair and a surprisingly unattractive face. She was sitting alone by one of the windows with a Dean Koontz novel in her hand. The girl who was with the ping-pong players still seemed to be waiting on whoever it was she was expecting. "You don't really seem like the kind of person who would ever want to do me wrong," he said at last.

"Neither do you," said Brandy.

"But we don't know each other."

"Exactly."

Albert continued to stare at the key.

"But so what if we're both telling the truth?" Brandy asked after a moment. "Then what? *Somebody* sent these things. *Somebody* scratched our names into them. That person knows what cars we drive, what classes we have, when we're in class and God only knows what else. So then who was it? Why would they do something like this? I'd rather think that *you* were trying to prank me. The fact that someone else out there is capable of this sort of stunt is way worse."

Albert could think of no reply for her. Come to think of it, how could anyone have known to leave that box in his car the previous night? It was the first time he'd ever driven to his night class. He didn't know until the previous weekend that the campus police stopped ticketing after five o'clock. *He* didn't even know he was going to drive until just before he left. He'd intended to drive only on rainy days, but he decided to see how much time it saved him.

That meant that someone must have been watching either him or his car that evening. The thought of a pair of eyes lurking unseen somewhere out there sent a shiver down his spine.

Two more students walked into the room together. One was a stout young man with short black hair and a thick, black goatee. The other was a rather plain-looking blonde girl with remarkably large breasts. The shorthaired girl stood up from the couch as they approached and greeted them both with a hug.

"So what do we do?" Brandy asked after a moment.

Albert held up the key. "I guess we open it," he replied. "We're both here. We have it. What can it hurt to open it and look inside? Maybe we'll figure out what it all means."

Brandy held onto the box, still not sure. She looked at the key for a moment, then looked up at Albert and said in a voice that was nearly a whisper, "What if it's a bomb or something?"

Albert hadn't considered a bomb. He stared down at the box, his thoughts whirling. Why would it be a bomb? But why not? Why crash airplanes into the World Trade Center? There was no end to the number of horrors that could be hidden in a box like this. He could almost imagine turning the key and watching it fly open as some hellish creature burst from within, its vicious jaws tearing the flesh from his body before he knew what was upon him.

He shook these thoughts away and met Brandy's eyes. "If it is," he decided at last, "we probably won't feel it."

Brandy's face paled at the thought of such an abrupt and brutal end. "I guess that's true," she said after a moment.

"With or without you," Albert said. "I think I have to open it. I have to know what's going on."

Brandy gazed back at him. "Why?"

"It's just who I am. I've always loved a good mystery. I read mysteries, I watch them, I can almost always figure out who did it." He looked down at the box. "This is the first *real* mystery I've ever come across. I guess I feel like, even if it's dangerous—stupid even—to open it, I want to." He shrugged and lowered his eyes. He felt foolish. "I feel like, above all else, I *want* this to be something real, you know?"

Brandy stared at him, surprised. "Yeah. I guess I do."

"I'm not saying we should. I don't know. Probably we shouldn't. I'm just saying I *want* to."

She nodded. "Okay." She moved the box closer to him, resting it on her knees, and then turned it so that the keyhole faced him. "I guess I do too."

He looked up at her, relieved that she understood him. He wanted to ask her if she was sure, but he didn't dare tempt her to reconsider. "Ready?"

Again, she nodded.

Slowly, Albert slid the key into the lock and began to turn it. For a moment he could feel the key searching for the slot—he still did not know which end was up—and then it fell into place and he felt the lock begin to turn. It moved sluggishly, as though stiff with age. When he had turned it a complete ninety degrees, a firm click announced that the lock was sprung and the key stopped in his fingers.

The two of them sat there for a moment, staring at the box. It was unlocked now, or at least they could only assume that it was, but they still didn't know how it was supposed to open.

"Now what?" Brandy asked, looking at Albert.

He did not know.

"I heard it unlock."

"So did I."

"So how does it open?"

He shook his head. "I don't know. I couldn't figure that out before when I was looking at it." He began to pull the key from the keyhole and after a moment of fumbling, the box began to open. It was now that it finally made sense to him. The box appeared seamless when he first examined it, except of course for those seams that one would expect to find in a wooden box, those where the wood was glued together. There were no hinges because the box did not have the kind of lid he'd been looking for. Instead, it consisted of two separate pieces, one inside the other. As he pulled the key out, the entire front side slid outward from the rest of the box.

"I see," Albert said. "It's like a drawer." It quickly became obvious that the box was lying on its side and he picked it up and turned it. Brandy's name was carved on the top of the box while part of the map made up the bottom.

"How'd you know to pull on the key like that?"

Albert glanced up at her. "I didn't. I was just trying to take it out."

She did not respond and Albert felt an odd sense of guilt. He could almost read her thoughts as she wondered if perhaps he'd been aware of how the box worked all along. "It's a really good fit," he observed, trying to keep her attention on the box itself. "You couldn't tell that the wood wasn't glued there, but it wasn't stuck closed, either." This was true. More true, in fact, than he cared to elaborate on. He pushed the box closed again for a moment and examined the seams. The fit was so perfect that there was not even the slightest movement when they were together, especially when the lock was turned. As he pulled it open again, he saw that there were small but formidable bolts on all four sides of the keyhole side of the inner box, and four no-doubt perfectly sized holes to receive the bolts in the outer box, like the deadbolt on a door, but four times as secure.

Still Brandy said nothing. Her silence felt like an accusation of some heinous crime for which he did not have an alibi.

Albert opened the box and peered inside. It would do no good to try and talk his way out of any suspicion. If she intended to blame him, there was nothing he could do to change her mind. The more he tried, the guiltier he would be perceived.

Besides, *he* knew he was innocent.

He hoped that opening the box would lead him to some answers, but as he gazed in at the contents, he quickly realized that there were only more questions within.

Random junk was all he found. There was a flat piece of rusted metal, a small stone, a dull metal object that he realized after a moment's consideration was a brass button, a dirty black feather and a silver pocket watch that might have been an antique, but was corroded far beyond any real value.

"What is all that?" Brandy asked, leaning forward until their foreheads were almost touching. "Does it mean anything?"

Albert shook his head. He did not know. He reached in and removed the watch. Its lid was loose, but still intact. Carved into the front was an elegant letter G. It was dirty, as were all the objects in the box, as though they had been dropped in mud at some point, and he used his thumb to clean the dirt from the design. Did the "G" indicate the owner of the watch, he wondered, or the company that manufactured it? Maybe he would look it up on the Internet sometime. He opened the cover and was surprised to find that the glass was still intact. Except for its apparent age, it was in surprisingly good condition. He found the stem and tried to wind it, half expecting it to start working again, but the insides had apparently not aged as well as the rest. The hands would not turn.

"Is it broken?"

Albert nodded. "Yeah." He handed it to her so that she could see it and then removed the feather. There was nothing very special about it. It wasn't from a very large bird. It was dirty and rather ratty-looking, like it was simply plucked from the gutter somewhere and dropped into the box.

Brandy placed the watch back into the box and removed the button. There were no distinguishing markings on it. It appeared to be a simple, old-fashioned brass button.

Albert dropped the feather back into the box and withdrew the stone. It was dark gray in color, about an inch in length, semi-cylindrical, with a strange texture. There were small creases along the sides. He rubbed away the dirt with his thumb and forefinger and saw that both ends were rough, as though it had been broken from a larger object.

Brandy dropped the button back into the box. "Does this stuff make any sense to you?"

"Not a bit." Albert dropped the stone back into the box and removed the final object. After turning it over in his fingers several times he concluded that it was the broken tip from some sort of knife. It was large enough to be from a dagger or a sword and, looking at the condition it was in, it certainly wasn't stainless steel. The original blade could have been just about anything.

"It's just junk."

"I know." Albert dropped the blade piece back into the box and fished out the button. As he examined it, four more people entered the room and sat down at the card table by the window. He recognized them immediately as the residents of the suite down the hall from his own. One of them was already shuffling a deck of cards and soon they would be immersed in a game. Albert saw them here often. Hearts seemed to be their game of choice, but he had already seen them play everything from Spades to Poker.

The room would only get more crowded as the night went on. By eight o'clock the only place that would be busier than the lounges was the computer room on the first floor. Albert tried to go there once just to check out the facilities, in case his own computer ever failed to meet his needs, and he was not even able to get in the door.

Brandy leaned back in the chair and looked sternly at Albert. "So what does it all mean then?"

"I don't know."

"Someone went to all the trouble of getting us together to open this fucking thing, so what are we supposed to get from it?"

Albert met her eyes for a moment and then dropped the button back into the box. He'd heard plenty of swearing in his life, as much from women as from men. Hell, his sister swore like a sailor when they were growing up. And he'd already heard Brandy swear plenty of times in the short time he'd been acquainted with her —she always seemed to be coming up with some delightfully creative expletive during their lab experiments—but it still surprised him somehow every time he heard something vulgar pass from her lips. She projected such a girlishly polite image that it was hard to imagine her as anything but young and innocent, virgin even. Of course, that wasn't to say that it was unattractive by any means. On the contrary, he actually found it to be something of a turn-on.

"I really don't know," he said after a moment. "You'd think there'd be something more."

Someone walked into the room and looked around, as though looking for someone. Albert glanced at her and recognized her as Gail from across the hall. He wondered vaguely if her presence here might indicate that Derek was no longer in her room. If so, he hoped he wasn't hanging out when he returned to *his* room. After a quick look around, Gail turned and left the lounge. Whoever she was looking for obviously wasn't here.

"This is ridiculous." Brandy closed the box, lifted it off her knees and dropped it into his lap. "I don't get it. I don't really care to get it." She grabbed her purse and stood up.

"What are you doing?"

"I'm leaving. You can keep all that. The key too. I'm

not interested."

Albert stared at her, surprised. "You're not even curious?"

She half turned as she slipped the thin strap of her purse over her shoulder. For a moment she paused, as though struggling with herself. "Yes," she said at last, her eyes fixed on the door. "If you come up with anything, let me know tomorrow in lecture."

"Okay." He could not believe she was just walking away from this. How could she? It was such a delicious mystery. Sure, the lack of answers inside the box was discouraging, even aggravating, but it was also all the more intriguing. These new questions were even more alluring than the first. How could anyone just walk away from such an enigma? Perhaps she was only being the more mature one, even the smarter one, but to just drop it and walk away? The very ability to do such a thing seemed so alien to him.

"I just don't like it," she explained before she walked away, as though she could feel the weight of his eyes and read the questions inside his head. "It's just... I don't know. It's just too much. I don't want to be a part of something I don't know anything about."

Albert nodded. He understood. It was probably the right thing to do. Nonetheless, he was disappointed.

"Bye." Brandy walked out of the room as a very pretty redhead entered and dropped into one of the soft chairs with a textbook.

Albert watched her go without getting up. It felt surprisingly sad knowing that this mystery was once again his alone.

Chapter 3

After leaving the second floor lounge, Albert slowly made his way back toward his room, his mind flooded with questions both old and new. He intended to go straight to his bed and lie down for a while, perhaps even retire for the night if his mind would take so long a break, but when he saw the door to his room standing wide open, he walked on by without pausing. He was in no mood for Derek this evening. He was particularly in no mood for Derek's horrible taste in television. Besides, right now he wanted to be alone with his thoughts.

He walked to the far end of the hallway, descended the stairs and then exited the building through the back doors. He did not have any particular destination in mind.

He merely wanted to take a walk, but he'd barely reached the steps when he remembered that he had not yet eaten dinner.

He crossed the street, climbed the steps of the University Center and then made his way downstairs to the cafeteria. This was where he'd eaten every meal since his arrival at Lumey. There was a larger cafeteria over in the Cube, where he'd been told the selection was far greater, but so far he'd seen no reason to walk halfway across campus when he was not yet bored with the menu here.

The dining area was pretty busy at this time of night, but it would be slowing down soon. Already the lines at the registers were beginning to shorten. Albert selected a cheeseburger, chips and a soda out of convenience—ham on a croissant from the sandwich shop would have been better, but he didn't feel like relaying his order to the lady at the counter—and then sought out a relatively private table at the far end of the room.

Often when he'd come here, the noise and the crowd would bother him, but tonight he actually enjoyed the atmosphere. Tonight, there was something very comforting about being alone in a room filled with people.

He unwrapped his cheeseburger and took a bite. He didn't feel terribly hungry. In fact, there was an unpleasant warmth in his belly, a sick sort of knot. He told himself he was merely tired, his mind overworked from trying to solve the riddles of the box all day, but he knew the feeling was mostly to do with Brandy.

That she could just walk away like that… How could she not want to know? How could she just leave and go about her life like nothing happened? He supposed she only did the responsible thing. Perhaps he was nothing more than a fool for thinking such a ridiculous box deserved such obsession, but he couldn't help it. The box was simply too intriguing to pass up. It was a riddle. And he'd always loved a good riddle. It was his thing. It was what he was good at. He was smart like that.

…Too smart to actually believe that this was really about any of that.

It was simple disappointment.

Still chewing his cheeseburger, he withdrew the key Brandy gave him from his jeans pocket and looked at it.

It was so simple; just a perfectly flat piece of metal, less than an eight of an inch thick, with no grooves of any kind. Only the simple shape of the teeth on either side allowed it to open the box, and yet the box itself was so finely crafted, with such an elaborate locking mechanism. The two just didn't seem to go together.

Sort of like he and Brandy, he supposed. But for just a few minutes...

A loud outburst from a few tables over drew him from his thoughts. He glanced over and surveyed the five people sitting there—two young men, three girls, all about the same age, perhaps a year ahead of him—and then turned his eyes back to his dinner.

He focused his concentration onto the key itself and began to review the things he'd found inside the box. The feather. The broken, rusted blade. The brass button. The silver pocket watch. The stone. What did they all mean? It all seemed like so much junk, but at the same time there was something else. There was something about them that tickled his brain, a strange sort of sense to be made from all the items in the box. It was a strange sort of sense in the simple fact that they made no sense. None of the things in the box fit together and that was exactly why the whole thing fit together. It was like a game, a tangled web of mysteries that each promised a key to solving the others. If someone meant it as a practical joke, they were good, and they knew him well enough to know that he'd be hooked. And this was precisely why he did not think that it was a practical joke.

It was strange, the way this kept drawing him in. He felt continuously compelled to return to the box, as if some unseen force was pushing him along, encouraging him to see the answers.

Once he was finished eating, he picked up the backpack and placed it in his lap. He intended to reach inside and open the box so that he could take another look at the items within, but as he reached for it, he caught sight of the carved words on one of the sides.

"Help," "Come Together" and "Yesterday." He'd almost forgotten. According to Brandy, these were all songs by The Beatles. Maybe the items inside the box weren't what he was supposed to gain from Brandy's visit. Maybe it was this small bit of knowledge. But what did it mean?

"Three songs," he muttered to himself, hardly aware that he was speaking aloud. Not just three songs, but three songs by the same group. That made it less likely to be a coincidence. If he'd been more into music, he might have made this connection as well, but he wasn't very familiar with the music of The Beatles.

Songs. Singing. Music. He read the last line to himself several times, the one that Brandy had not recognized:

G N J

Albert stood up, slipped the backpack over his shoulders and walked away from the table. He no longer noticed the people around him. He threw away his garbage on his way out of the cafeteria and then climbed the stairs and left the building heading south across campus. The three song titles circled again and again through his thoughts. Music. Perhaps it was a long shot, but just maybe whoever carved those song titles into the box was referring to the university's music building.

The music building was on the other side of campus,

next to the field house. Albert made his way south on Third Street, then west on Pole Street, which passed by the Cube. The Cube was four identical eight-story dormitories built together in a square. This was the main dormitory on campus, where better than half of all the resident students lived. He passed the Cube, crossed Redwood Avenue and then left Pole heading south on a sidewalk that took him past the art building and the field house to the music building.

Albert walked around to the front, taking in his surroundings as he walked, and paused in front of the main doors. There was a large sign over the door, proclaiming the building as Juggers Hall. Until he arrived here, he hadn't been able to remember the name of the music building.

Juggers.

He stepped through the front doors and found himself in an empty lobby. His hunch was growing into something more certain and he was able to find what he was looking for immediately. On one of the walls, hanging over a row of chairs that looked soft and cozy, but probably weren't, was a large portrait of a balding, silver-haired gentleman in an expensive suit. He wore a thick mustache and an air of kind authority. Beneath the portrait, on an engraved plate, was the name Dr. George Nicholas Juggers.

George Nicholas Juggers.

G. N. J.

He'd found it.

He sat down beneath George Nicholas Juggers—his hunch about the coziness of the chairs was correct—and opened his backpack. "Help," "Come Together" and "Yesterday" were song titles, and the GNJ referred to this building. Albert turned the box in his hands. First Brandy. He'd shown the box to Brandy and when Brandy found the key, she brought it to him. More important than the key, however, was that she'd brought him the answer to the second clue. Songs. He'd made the connection between song titles and music and followed his instincts to the music building, where he was rewarded with the third clue. Now he knew where to look. And what he was looking for were those last three lines. An I and a Z—or was it a *one* and a Z? The second line still looked like a roman numeral seven, but there was no way of knowing for sure. And the last line could've been anything.

He stood up and looked around the room. There were soda machines against the wall and an elevator machine room in one corner, two tables and about a dozen of those falsely cozy chairs, but there was nothing that appeared to match any of the markings on the box. He spent several minutes pacing around the room, examining everything, but there was nothing there.

His first thought was that the songs narrowed it down to the building and the initials narrowed it down to the room, but maybe the initials were just another part of the previous clue. He set off down the hallway, peering into any rooms that were open or that offered windows through which he could see. He took the stairs up to the second and then third floor and then took the elevator down to the basement.

Nothing.

Eventually he found his way around to the back of the building and he stepped outside. Perhaps the next day he would tell Brandy what he'd found and she could help him determine what the last clues meant. Already the janitors who were vacuuming the carpets up on the third floor were beginning to give him strange looks. He could hardly blame them. He was creeping around like a thief looking for something to steal, cradling a strange wooden box in his arms. He'd be lucky if they didn't call campus security on him.

He was about to walk back into the building for one last look around when something caught his eye.

No, that wasn't right. It didn't catch his eye. It was as though something *compelled* him to turn and look back, as though a soft voice had whispered from that direction, begging him to turn and see.

For a moment he didn't see anything, just the sidewalk, some trees, the billowing white smoke of the power plant beyond, the darkening sky above. There was nothing out of the ordinary, nothing he couldn't see walking out of any other building. But then he saw it, right there in plain sight, yet well hidden. He'd walked past so many of them. They were all over campus. It was the panic button.

These big red buttons were attached to six-foot posts all over campus and wired directly to the campus security headquarters in the administration building. In the event of an emergency, one push of this button would bring the campus police rushing to this location.

There were dozens of these buttons on campus, but no two were exactly identical. They each displayed a different number above the button, identifying the station. This particular button was number twelve.

It wasn't a Z at all. It was a number two. A one and a two. *Twelve*.

Albert felt certain that this was the first of the three clues on this final side of the box, but he felt neither excited nor proud to have found it. Instead, he suddenly felt very creepy. What made him turn and look at the panic button in the first place? It was as though something reached into his head and *made* him see it.

No. That was preposterous. He simply saw it immediately, registered it subconsciously and then reacted to it a moment later. That was all.

Still, something felt very weird. Perhaps it wasn't right. He walked over to the button and examined it. Except for the number twelve and the warning sign that hung beneath it, there was nothing. He turned and looked around him, convinced that this was the wrong solution after all. But then he found the second clue staring down at him from the roof of Juggers Hall. A tower rose up from the center of the roof and a large clock-face stared back at him. On that clock face, directly between roman numerals six and eight, was the second clue.

Albert stared up at the clock, unable to believe what he saw. What he did next he did almost without thinking. Standing in front of the number twelve panic button, he stared up at the clock and traced a straight line with his eyes from the center of the clock, past the seven and down to the ground. There, set into the concrete was a large metal plate, an entrance to the tunnel that ran beneath the sidewalk.

He walked over to this metal covering and found the final clue. Near one corner, a number was stamped into the metal:

1005T

There was no way to know what that number meant, or how to read it. This particular chunk of metal could have been manufactured almost anywhere in the world. It could have been designed for anything and then salvaged and used here as a way to keep students from trespassing. But here it was, looking him in the face, the answer to the riddle of the box.

The tunnels. The map that made up the last two sides of the box could only be of the steam tunnels beneath the campus.

He looked back up at the building in front of him. Finding this number should have excited him, but instead the discovery disturbed him. The number on the plate was so absolute, so distinctive, that there was no denying that it was exactly where the box was leading him. Where else would he find 1005T? But the clues leading up to it were so subtle. Sure the first four words spelled out song titles, even titles all belonging to a single band, a very popular band, no less, but it seemed like such a leap of faith to jump from related song titles to the campus music building. Why did it not occur to him instead to check the music store at the mall, or to look the Beatles up on the Internet? Or why not find those three songs and listen to them, or look up the lyrics to see if they had anything in common? He was very talented at solving puzzles and riddles, so why was his only thought the campus music building?

The initials, he thought. *G. N. J.* Every building on campus was named after someone. The Craw Building was named after William Craw. Wuhr was named after Daniel Wuhr. His dormitory was named after Walter Lumey. Initials led to a name, a name led to a building, a building having something in common with music...

No. It was too much of a leap, too doubtful. If the location of this metal cover was actually meant to be found, whoever encrypted it had placed an enormous amount of faith in his ability to make such a connection. After all, when he thought of the music building he didn't think of *songs* so much as *instruments*. He thought of marching bands, not rock bands.

And presuming he *did* actually make the connection, it took an even greater leap of faith to expect him to spot the number twelve from the back door of the building, especially when he was looking for a Z.

Maybe that was precisely the point. Maybe whoever sent the box intended for the puzzle to be too difficult to solve.

Albert frowned at this idea. That made even less sense. Why send the box at all then? No, that wasn't logical in the least. He looked up at the clock face. Perhaps whoever carved the number into the box did not think about his two being mistaken for a Z. Would the number twelve have been such a hard thing to find if he'd known what he was looking for? Somehow he doubted it. Twelve was a relatively common number. It probably appeared dozens of times in and around the building. *Room* twelve was one example.

Most unlikely of all, he realized, was the understanding that one needed to actually stand in front of the post with the number on it and recognize the seven o'clock digit as an arrow pointing away from the center of the clock face toward an inconspicuous metal plate set into the sidewalk several yards from the nearest corner of the building. Shouldn't his first thought have been to try and find a way into the clock tower to look for the final clue? Or to make some sort of numerical or symbolic connection with the number seven or the seven o'clock hour?

He remembered the strange double-take he'd done to

recognize the panic button, as if something had whispered into his very brain. He tried to remember exactly what it was that made him look again, but he couldn't quite recall.

This wasn't how he usually thought his way through a puzzle. The solutions came in logical steps, not gut feelings. He followed a path, unlocked the clues...

He forced the idea out of his head and stuffed the box back into his backpack. That was stupid. He'd just gotten lucky, that was all. He'd found the solution quickly instead of turning up a hundred dead ends before locating the tunnel entrance. But all the way back to Lumey, he kept glancing back over his shoulder, half expecting someone to be watching him.

Chapter 4

The creepiness that Albert felt that evening behind Juggers Hall was gone before he fell asleep that night and by the next morning he couldn't wait to see what was in those tunnels.

He spent the morning planning, trying to decide the best way to proceed. He needed some supplies. Flashlights for sure, with plenty of extra batteries, and it wouldn't hurt to have a plan to keep from getting lost.

It was maddening. He grew more and more eager to see what mysteries waited beneath the sidewalks. If the map on the box was true, then it was certainly more than just a simple steam tunnel stretching out from the power plant. It would have to be connected directly to the city sewer system, and even then the tunnels would have to be much more complicated than a city this size would really require. The map itself was simply a set of lines depicting only the path he would be taking, but along the way there were dozens of short lines branching off the main path, suggesting intersections that could lead anywhere. It seemed like so much for a city where the college made up a fair percentage of the population. He wondered if there was something hidden down there, something fantastic.

He drove to the local Wal-Mart and purchased his supplies, preparing himself for what he was sure would be a fantastic adventure. And later, before lecture, he told Brandy of his discoveries, only to be brought back to earth with a resounding crash.

"The *sewers*?"

"Well, not *sewers*," Albert replied, already sure of what she was thinking. "They're *some* sort of tunnels. They're probably connected to the sewers somewhere, but I think they're mostly service tunnels running from the power plant. Steam tunnels, probably."

"That's crazy."

"Maybe. But who knows."

Brandy did not reply. She was searching the contents of her purse for some lip-gloss.

"You in?"

She turned and looked at him as though he'd lost his mind. "What do you mean am I 'in'?"

"I mean I'd like to go down there and look around. I want to see where the map takes us."

She gave him a look that was all she needed to say, her eyes narrowed, her nose wrinkled, a genuine "are you nuts" expression if ever he'd seen one. "No way."

Albert looked down at his notebook. She'd succeeded in making him feel perfectly silly.

"I don't care if there's a million dollars in gold and jewels down there, I wouldn't wade through sewage for anything." She went back to looking for her lip-gloss. "Besides, what makes you sure there's anything down there anyway?"

"Maybe there's not. Maybe there is. Weirder shit's happened."

"Touché."

"I bought some supplies. I think it's worth a look."

"You're crazy. Somebody gave us that box to get us

to go down there. I don't know about you, but I wouldn't care much for the thought of being underground in the dark, maybe too far down for anyone to hear me screaming, and knowing that somebody *I don't know* knows I'm down there."

Albert nodded. He couldn't really argue that logic.

"This isn't the world's safest campus, you know. Remember a couple of years ago when two students disappeared?"

"I hadn't heard about that."

"One in the winter, one in the spring. Never found. Somebody else was murdered a year or two before that, too. A girl. Raped and strangled. They found her in the bushes near the Cube."

"Wow."

"Yeah. They all could have received a mysterious box, too."

Albert could think of no reply. She was right, of course. He remembered that weird paranoia he'd felt after he located the tunnel entrance. He wondered again at the odds of correctly solving the clues in such a short amount of time.

Brandy had been speaking to him, but not looking at him. Now she turned and looked directly at him, her blue eyes brilliant. "Just stay above ground, okay? You're a nice guy. Don't get yourself killed."

That pretty much settled it. After class he came home and sat down at his desk. He felt like a first class idiot. He'd spent good money on flashlights and batteries, and all for a stupid expedition that made no sense to anyone but himself. There was no proof that there was anything down there. There was nothing but a map and a box full of junk. Furthermore, she was absolutely right when she said that somebody gave them the box, somebody whose intentions had obviously been for them to follow the map, but who neglected to mention *why*. In a country where there were something like thirty-five serial killers active at any given time and somewhere someone turned up missing, raped, brutalized or murdered almost hourly, it was far more likely that such a map would lead to a sociopath than to a treasure.

Above all, Albert Cross was a logical-minded person, and he could not deny that, logically, nothing about the box made any sense.

That night, he took the box with all its contents, locked it and then placed it and the key inside the plastic bag with the things he'd bought that morning. He then dropped the entire box into his bottom desk drawer and closed it.

Chapter 5

On the following Monday, Albert arrived at class early, and was sitting at the table when Brandy walked in. She was wearing a small, purple dress, and he was surprised by how great it looked on her. Her slender legs were smooth and sexy, her figure lean, modest, pretty. She dropped her backpack on the table and sat down next to him, her knees neatly together, perfectly ladylike.

"Hello," she chimed with tired cheerfulness.

"Hi. You look nice today."

"Thanks." She smiled at him as she sat down, genuinely pleased by his compliment.

"Special occasion or just wanted to dress nice?"

"Just wanted to."

"That's cool. If you know you're pretty, show it."

She smiled at him again, this time with a shy sort of embarrassment. He had flattered her. The look made him blush a little.

"You going to be ready for Friday's test?" she asked, mercifully changing the subject.

"I think so. How about you?"

"Tests always make me nervous, but we'll see."

"I've always liked tests. Usually means no homework."

"That's true."

"I'm going into the tunnels."

Brandy looked at him so quickly that she nearly startled him. "What?"

"I'm going. I've been thinking about it all weekend." Obsessing over it was more like it. He hadn't been able to stop wondering where the box came from and what it meant. He could not get it off his mind. He kept finding himself gazing toward his desk, toward the drawer where it was hidden away. "I have to know what's down there and I have to know why that stuff was sent to us."

"Albert, I don't know."

"I know. I'm just telling you because this belongs to you too. If you don't want to come that's fine, I understand, but I can't go down there without at least letting you know I'm going. Give you the option."

"I'm not going."

"Okay."

"I really don't think it's a good idea."

"I know."

"It's not safe."

"I'm going tonight. If you don't see me again, you'll know that for sure."

"Don't say that. It's scary."

"I'm sorry."

She shook her head. "Crazy."

"I know."

She began to remove her books from her backpack. "I mean I want to know what's down there too, but *Jesus*."

"I'll let you know tomorrow."

Brandy laughed. It was a short bark of a laugh, the sort of laugh that was akin to rolling ones eyes. "What is it with boys and adventures?"

"Too many cartoons."

Again she laughed, this time more freely. "Yeah. I think so."

"If you decide you want to come along, that's fine. I've got two flashlights. Otherwise, I'm fine solo too."

Brandy looked at him without speaking. Something stirred in her eyes, something he did not quite understand, but thought was a struggle. A part of her wanted to go, he could tell, she wasn't really trying very hard to talk him out of it, after all, but it was only a small part of her. He hadn't expected her to go, and why should she? Look at her. She was a beautiful young woman. He did not very well picture her crawling through dirty tunnels.

"No pressure," he promised.

She said nothing more about the matter, and when class was over, she quickly gathered her things and left ahead of him.

Albert was disappointed. It would have been nice to have her along. It would have been sort of like a date, although a terribly unromantic one. He stuffed his books into his backpack, taking his time, and started home.

He'd done his best to invite Brandy on this

adventure. He'd wanted her company, to spend some time alone with her. He had hoped that they would be able to get to know each other a little better. But it was also the right thing to do. He felt that whatever was down there belonged as much to her as to him, and he would not have wanted *her* to set off into the tunnels without *him*. And if she was right about the dangers, then at least someone would know where he'd gone if he didn't make it back.

Besides, he'd already known that she would likely refuse the offer. He'd already resigned himself to proceeding without her. This was why it came as such a surprise when he found Brandy waiting for him outside the main doors, a cigarette in one hand, the other clinging to the strap of her bag. Her hair whipped across her face in the breeze and she squinted against the bright sunlight. She didn't look at him, but rather out at the sprawling campus around them.

"I just know I'm going to regret this," she said.

Chapter 6

They met on the back steps of Juggers Hall. Some research had revealed to Albert that this was the business building up until the construction of the new Craw Building a few years earlier. Now it was the music building.

Albert arrived first, dressed in blue jeans and a long sleeve shirt and wearing his bulky, green backpack. It was a little chilly, but he chose to leave his jacket at home. He counted on being out of the wind and doing a lot of walking. Brandy arrived shortly after, dressed in jeans, tennis shoes and a dark blue sweatshirt. Her purse was slung over one shoulder. It wasn't as sexy as the dress she'd been wearing that afternoon, but she was no less lovely.

Albert had told her to meet him here at midnight. From here they would slip into the service tunnel by way of the entrance he'd found. Even on a Monday night, there would be people out at all hours on a university campus, but he counted on the traffic being light by midnight. It would have been safer to wait until after two or three, but then they ran some risk of surfacing in the morning when traffic on the sidewalk would be terrible. The university would not take well to students walking around in their steam tunnels. It was likely a major violation.

The area was deserted. Two girls passed by just after Albert first arrived, but he'd seen no one since. There was no traffic to worry about. There were no roads within sight and from here all the buildings stood with their backs to them. No lights shined in any windows, the custodians either at work elsewhere in the buildings or, more likely, finished for the night. Luck was with them.

"Well," announced Brandy, not sure what to say. "I'm here."

"Yes you are." Albert was looking around, checking

again for anyone who might have crept near enough to see them, but the area was still deserted. It was almost eerie in its still silence. During the day this area bustled with foot traffic almost continuously.

"So now what?"

"Now we go down." He descended the steps and crossed the wide sidewalk to the tunnel entrance. He looked around one last time and then knelt and pulled at the cover. It was heavy as hell, more so than he expected. For a moment he thought it was going to prove too heavy for him to open, and the thought was maddening. If he couldn't move this cover, then what could they possibly do? It was the only way in that he knew about, and even if he did find another entrance, he was certain the map started right here. He hadn't been able to find any information at all about these tunnels online, much less a map.

He repositioned himself and tried again. This time the cover moved, but not without a great deal of effort. It slid across the concrete, grinding with enough noise, it seemed, to be heard from at least Memphis, but no one came to see what he was doing. When the cover was pushed far enough over to allow them to enter, he stopped to catch his breath and peered into the thick darkness below. Warm air rose up to meet his face and suddenly he was struck by the magnitude of what he was doing.

Up until now he'd been single-mindedly playing along with the box, contemplating the mystery first and his doubts second. But now he was taking a fabulous risk. He was getting ready to trespass in what was undoubtedly very restricted university property. If he and Brandy were caught in these tunnels, they would almost certainly face very serious charges. They could be expelled. They could be handed over to the city police and arrested. In his need to follow these clues he had managed to put both himself and Brandy in a very vulnerable position. And yet, Brandy had ultimately chosen to come with him of her own free will.

"Something wrong?"

Albert glanced up at her and then quickly looked around. Still no one had appeared. "Just catching my breath," he replied. "Want me to go first?"

Brandy nodded quickly. He could tell she was

nervous about going down there, and he didn't blame her.

"Okay." An iron ladder was bolted to the concrete on one wall of the tunnel. He placed his backpack on the ground next to it and climbed carefully into the darkness. He paused once to withdraw one of the flashlights from the bag and then descended into the tunnel.

For a brief moment he stood in the darkness, feeling the humid atmosphere. He knew that the tunnel stretched some distance in both directions, probably at least the full length of the sidewalk, and he allowed himself only that moment to feel the vulnerability of his blindness before turning on the flashlight.

"Hand me the backpack."

Brandy knelt down beside the hole and lowered the bag down to him.

Albert took it and slid his arms through the straps. "Okay. Come on down. Watch your step."

"Someone's coming."

"*What?*"

"Turn off the flashlight!"

Albert obeyed without delay. In an instant he was swallowed by darkness. He looked up through the opening above the ladder and saw that Brandy had vanished. Voices rose from the direction of the field house.

In the darkness, Albert felt terribly vulnerable. He wasn't able to examine the tunnel very well in the short time the flashlight was on, but he'd seen enough to give his imagination plenty to work with. The tunnel stretched beyond the reach of the beam in both directions. Huge pipes ran the entire length of one wall while thick bundles of cables snaked along the other. Overhead was a freeway of water pipes. A locked switchbox of some sort was mounted near the ladder. The only other things he'd seen were concrete and shadows. The air was musty and warm. Far ahead he could see a narrow, dim light casting eerie, motionless shadows across the wall and lamplight drifted through a number of grates in the sidewalk. There was a grumbling of distant machinery that suddenly sounded like the snoring of some enormous beast. Standing alone in the darkness, it was far too easy to imagine things slinking toward him, nasty, drooling things with teeth and claws. The walls began to close; the cables and pipes unfastened themselves and reached out for him. Claustrophobia crept over him and childhood terrors rose from long dormant chambers of his mind.

The voices grew closer, more audible. Boys. At least two of them. He could not hear the subject of their conversation, but he heard when the subject changed.

"Whoa! Watch out." One voice. Deep. Smooth.

"Yeah, *that's* not dangerous at all." Another voice, this one lighter. Softer.

Shadows passed over the opening and the voices faded. Somebody changed the subject, a third voice, he thought, but wasn't sure. It could have been the first again. He focused on their voices, tried to picture the people they belonged to and wondered how different they really were from what he imagined.

He didn't like being blind. Without the ability to view his surroundings, he was at the mercy of his imagination, and his imagination could be surprisingly frightening. And he hated being frightened. Fear was an illogical reaction to things like this. Fear should be reserved for human cruelty and natural disasters, not for empty, dark corridors. Standing in the darkness now, he thought he could almost feel the fur of some snarling creature brushing against the leg of his pants.

When the voices were completely gone he concentrated on the box and on his plan. The boys changing the subject meant that the open entrance to the tunnel was already forgotten. They probably assumed that it was left open by a forgetful maintenance worker or by some kids goofing around.

After what seemed like hours, he heard more footsteps. Then another shadow fell across the opening and Brandy's voice drifted down to him like the welcome ring of rescue vehicles to a disaster scene. "They're gone."

Albert snapped on the flashlight with all the force of a drowning man gasping for air. Light filled the tunnel again, mercifully chasing away the darkness and revealing not a single drooling creature. There was not even a small rat to blame his irrationality on. As always when he found himself relieved of such situations where his imagination overpowered his senses, he felt embarrassed. It seemed to him that Brandy must be able to see him blush, that he must have his silly childishness written across his face in brilliant red hues.

"I couldn't cover the hole. I just started walking. Went right past them and they didn't even notice me. I went up past the field house and circled back." She eased down onto the ladder and began to descend. She sounded out of breath. "I think they noticed the hole."

"Yeah, but they didn't think much about it." Her quick thinking impressed Albert. He might have tried to run and hide and most certainly would have attracted their curiosity. "We should be fine."

Once Brandy was off the ladder, Albert handed her the flashlight and then climbed up and slid the cover noisily back into place. It was a little bit easier from down here. Gravity worked with him more. When they were effectively sealed in, he removed the second flashlight, a can of spray paint and the box from the backpack and slipped it on again. With only the extra batteries inside, it was much lighter.

"That was really cool, actually," Brandy remarked as he fumbled with the backpack. The girlish excitement in her voice lifted his spirits and helped to settle his nerves from his time in the dark. "I haven't done anything like this since I was a little girl."

"Did you sneak into a lot of tunnels when you were a kid?"

Brandy smiled. "Sort of. My cousins and I used to sneak into our grandma's basement when no one was looking. We weren't supposed to be down there, but it was so cool and creepy. It had this narrow little stairway and the floor was always a little muddy." Those days seemed so far away now. It had been four or five years since she'd really spent any time with any of her cousins. She was the youngest of the five and they were all grown up now. The others were all married or engaged. It was kind of sad. Thinking back on it now, it felt less like she'd outgrown her childhood and more like life had outgrown her.

Albert chuckled at the thought of her creeping around in an old basement. "Sounds like some of the stuff I used to do." He thought of his grandparents' farm. The old, leaning barn. The cellar. Plenty of places he wasn't supposed to go, but always did. That was so long ago. Could he possibly already be so old as to have such distant memories?

"I guess that's part of the reason I wanted to do this,"

Brandy said. "It makes me feel like a kid on a big adventure." She gazed around wonderingly. It was a warm feeling, getting that old jolt she remembered from her childhood adventures.

"I wondered what changed your mind."

She shrugged. "I don't know. I still think this is kind of stupid."

It *was* stupid. If anyone caught them down here there'd be hell to pay one way or another.

"What do you suppose this tunnel's for anyway?" She was looking back toward the field house. A few yards beyond the ladder there were some steps leading down and a tangle of pipes and valves near the floor.

"Steam tunnel." He examined the map on the two sides of the box, trying to determine which end was the beginning. "Probably runs from the power plant to Juggers and the field house. I think all the electric, water, phone and networking lines run through tunnels like these, along with heat in the form of steam through these big pipes. Hence the term '*steam tunnel*'." He looked toward the steps for a moment and then turned and looked back the other way. He wondered if that distant light was coming from the power plant. "I don't really know for certain, though. I tried to look it up online and couldn't find anything about Briar Hills."

"I'm sure the university doesn't really want to advertise its tunnels. I doubt if they'd be too thrilled to find us down here."

Albert nodded. "Yeah. These things are dangerous. I didn't find anything about Briar Hills, but I found some information on other steam tunnels. Lots of campuses use them. The one thing they all seem to have in common is that they all have confined spaces and extremely hot temperatures. There's a very real threat of heat stroke and severe burns from the machinery down here."

Brandy was looking around nervously now. "Will we be in trouble if somebody catches us?"

"Probably."

"You could've told me about this *before* we came down here."

"Would it have changed your mind?"

"Yes." But she realized even as she replied that it probably wouldn't have. In fact, it probably would have made the adventure even *more* appealing. Although she probably would have dressed differently.

"I'm sorry." Albert looked back down at the map, turning it this way and that, trying to read it. "Hopefully this will keep us away from all the really dangerous areas." *If I can figure out how to read it*, he thought. It was made up entirely of straight lines. A single line stretched around the corner of the box, making sudden sharp turns as it went. Most of the time, another line continued forward a short distance from each turn and then stopped, suggesting that the tunnel went on ahead, but was of no importance. Along the way, other lines jutted off the main path and stopped, showing other tunnels that should be passed by. Aside from this network of straight lines, there were no markings on the map. There was no start, no finish, not even an X marks the spot. "It doesn't say which way's up," he observed, "but I figure if we go the wrong way we won't get far before the map stops making sense."

Brandy nodded. She couldn't stop thinking about what might happen if somebody caught them down here. How much trouble would they be in? What would her parents say?

"Let's try this way." He nodded toward the power plant and then handed her the spray paint can. "That's for marking the walls as we go. It'll help us find our way back out if we get lost."

"Good idea." Brandy took the can and shook it.

"Sorry. I'd carry it, but the map's a little awkward."

"I understand."

They began to walk east through the tunnel, away from the field house. Above them, dim light glowed where the drainage grates were located, a reminder that the world was only a few feet overhead and not lost forever. Albert's eyes kept lifting to these. From up there, the glow of their flashlights must be visible. He hoped nobody noticed them.

"There should be a left right up here."

The light did not penetrate far in the dark tunnels, but the words were barely out of his mouth when he saw the passage appear up ahead. "So far so good."

"Great." Brandy removed the lid from the spray paint can and shook it.

"Make it subtle. No sense advertising to the maintenance crews that we were here."

She marked the wall with a soft curving line, a sort of subtle arrow indicating the turn. "How far do you think it is?"

"Hard to say. The map's not really well scaled." He shined his flashlight farther up the tunnel toward the power plant and caught sight of an iron gate blocking access to a passage leading to the right. A chain and padlock prevented anyone from passing. He assumed that all access to any of the campus buildings would be similarly barricaded. He was a little surprised that they'd gained entry so easily.

The next tunnel sloped slightly downhill. The large pipes continued on along the previous tunnel, but some of the cables and smaller pipes had turned with them. He wished he knew more about these tunnels. He hated not knowing where he was going.

About forty feet ahead, Albert spied a crevice in the left wall. As they approached it, he realized that there was a square hole in this crevice and a steel ladder to carry them down. He peered into the hole and saw that the tunnel below ran at an odd angle to the one they were currently in and matched exactly with the one the map described, which was good because about four yards in front of him was another iron gate bound with chains and a padlock.

"Looks like we go down," he said, shining his light into the darkness below.

"You sure?" Brandy was gazing down into the hole. Dusty white cobwebs crisscrossed the narrow passage. She watched with disgust as a particularly fat spider scurried beneath one of the ladder rungs.

"I'm not really sure about anything, to be perfectly honest."

Chapter 7

The tunnels beneath Briar Hills weren't like the sewers on television. Although he knew that Briar Hills in no way required the vast subterranean systems that New York City warranted, he nonetheless had pictured the wide, gloomy corridors with rounded ceilings that were so often depicted on television. What he found instead were confined, concrete passageways, many of them too short to allow them to walk without stooping. Shortly after their descent from the second passage, they were forced to continue on hands and knees beneath massive bundles of cables.

There was water everywhere. A perpetual dampness permeated the concrete around them, so that soon the knees of their jeans were soaked through. Shallow pools of standing water stretched along the floor in many of the tunnels, and the hollow echo of dripping water was as common as the shadows.

But nothing down here was constant, not even the sounds. At times there was a strumming of machinery echoing around them and at other times the tunnels were silent as tombs. Several times they were startled by strange noises they knew was the natural gurgling of water through some machine or some other harmless thing, perhaps even the simple flushing of a toilet somewhere above them, but which sounded like the gargling moans of something unearthly in the shadows. And several times there were skittering, scuffling noises that very likely did belong to something alive and hungry (but almost certainly small and harmless).

At one point they stepped out into a large, open tunnel with an enormous pipe running along the center of the floor. Here the machinery was the loudest and the temperature the hottest. But there were lights in this tunnel, and the floor was dry for a change. It was a welcome passage while they traveled it, but too soon the map told them to exit into a passage on the right and they found themselves in another damp corridor that took them to another rusty ladder that waited to take them deeper into the darkness.

From here, the floors became muddier, the walls slimier, and soon it became apparent to Albert that they were no longer in the university steam tunnels. It had been some time since they saw or heard any kind of machinery and the overall feel of the tunnels was different now. They found long stretches of round, concrete passages with few intersections. A few times they heard cars passing somewhere overhead and once they heard voices drifting from drainage grates in an adjoining tunnel, but for the most part they felt completely isolated from the world above them.

The worst part about these newer tunnels was the cobwebs. These rarely used passages were a haven for spiders of all types. Ghostly white curtains wavered at their approach, casting odd shadows across the walls. At times it looked to Albert like a city of pale silk, as if the tiny creatures had discovered a place private enough to build a metropolis. Invisible, gossamer strands licked their faces and clung to their clothes as they passed, and several times Brandy cried out in revulsion as one of the arachnid inhabitants of the silken city danced across the exposed skin of her face or hands.

"These tunnels just go on forever," Brandy observed.

Albert nodded agreement. "I know. This city's not that big. It seems like overkill." The steam tunnels he'd expected. He was sure they snaked beneath the entire campus, perhaps for many miles, reaching as far as the river, and even several levels deep. But it felt to him that they'd already traveled enough tunnels to stretch from one end of the city to the other and back again. He'd begun to wonder if the entire city followed the university's example, tying together the courthouse and the police station or the library and post office, perhaps networking the entirety of the city's public buildings. But much of what they saw contained no equipment of any kind. It had even been a while since he last saw any cables or pipes. And yet, the labyrinth-like system didn't seem like a very efficient sewer system. He would have thought that most of the tunnels would point east, toward the Mississippi River, but they seemed to go every which way. The tunnel they were in now didn't look like it had ever held water. He wondered if some of these tunnels were a flood-prevention system of some kind, perhaps designed to carry large amounts of water past the city in the event that the mighty river overflowed its banks, as it was certainly known to do.

"I've always heard rumors about old tunnels under the city."

Albert glanced at her, curious.

"There're supposed to be miles and miles of them. Real old. Some people say they're haunted."

"Really?"

"Yeah. There's lots of stories. Witches and voodoo. That sort of thing. Some people say that the city's founders were into witchcraft. Used to scare the shit out of me when I was a girl." She was looking around, uneasy at the thought. "I haven't thought about those stories in ages. I figured they were all made up."

"Sometimes there's truth behind myths."

"Yeah. I heard a friend of my parents tell them once that some of the tunnels were older than the city itself. He said no one knows how they got there." She chuckled softly. "Daddy always said he was full of shit."

Albert smiled. "Sometimes stories like that are comforting. Some people have a hard time believing that there aren't any more mysteries left in the world. I guess I'm one of them."

Brandy looked at him and smiled. "That's kind of romantic."

"Is it?"

"Yeah." She turned and looked down the dark tunnel ahead. "But right now I'd rather not believe that there are secret tunnels built by centuries-old witches, if you don't mind."

Albert laughed. "Of course. I won't bring it up again. But you have to promise to tell me more about those stories when we get out of here."

"It's a deal." She smiled at him and he felt a sort of warmth flow from her. He couldn't help but wonder what she was thinking.

They turned right and found a set of concrete steps descending deeper into the earth. At the bottom was another iron gate, this one different from those back in the university steam tunnels. Instead of a chain, it was secured by a simple latch and a place for a padlock. There was no lock present, however, and the gate stood ajar, as though waiting for them. Beyond the gate was a small room. There were a number of discarded soda cans and an old furnace filter lying among a scattering of cigarette butts, yellow insulation shreds and twisted strips of rusty metal. There were holes in the walls varying in size from one to eight inches in diameter, suggesting that there used to be pipes running through this room, perhaps even a heating system of some kind. Directly across from them was a heavy door with no handle.

"Where do you suppose that goes?" Brandy wondered aloud.

Some basement was Albert's guess. Or maybe the basement of a basement. But he wasn't interested in the door. There was obviously no way to open it and it wasn't on the map. He shrugged and set his eyes on the left side of the room, where a rusty railing separated them from a twelve-foot drop. Another rusty ladder led down into the lower space where another open gate waited.

Brandy crossed the room and studied the door. It was bolted shut so tightly that it didn't even rattle when she pushed on it. It could have been nailed shut, for all she knew. She put her ear to it and listened for a moment, but it was silent on the other side.

"It's one o'clock in the morning," Albert said. "Unless it opens right into the party room at one of the frat houses, I doubt you'll hear anything."

Brandy shot him a curt look. "There might have been machines or something."

"That's true," he admitted.

"Thank you."

"Come on. We're getting closer."

They descended the ladder and continued on. Left at the bottom of the ladder. Right some distance beyond that, past one intersection and then right again at the next.

"So what do you think we're going to find down here, anyway?" Brandy asked as she lit a cigarette.

Albert shrugged. "I don't know."

"You haven't even imagined?"

"Not really." It was the truth. He spent so much time trying to solve the puzzles and figuring out how to follow the map, that he really hadn't thought much about where it might lead them, only that it must lead *somewhere*. He hoped it would be something fantastic enough to make all this worth it.

Brandy paused to mark the wall again and Albert glanced back at her. "You're the one who was so intent on coming down here. Tell me what you think we'll find when we get there."

"I really don't know."

"Humor me." She turned and set her soft eyes on his. There was playfulness in her expression, but there was something else there as well. Albert thought she was testing him, trying to feel him out for something. A lie, perhaps.

"A treasure chest?" he offered. "Some ancient scrolls? A big X and a shovel? Regis Philbin and a studio audience?"

Brandy smiled, but he could tell she wasn't really amused. "Come on. What is it you really *want* to find down here?"

Albert frowned. What did he *want* to find? What kind of question was that? Did it really matter what they found?

Brandy stood and watched him for a moment while

she smoked, waiting for his answer.

"I don't know," he said again.

"Really?" She continued to watch him for a moment. Albert watched her watch him, unsure of what else to say. He'd already told her he didn't know. Finally, she looked off down the darkened tunnel as if daydreaming and said, "I think it would be awesome if we found a lost vault. Maybe a gangster's hideout." She turned her brilliant eyes back to him. "Someone like Al Capone, you know." She looked down at her cigarette and was silent for a moment as she pondered the thought. "Imagine a cramped little room with a gas lantern on a table and a stack of stolen money from a bank heist." She looked up at him again and the youthful fascination in her eyes was mesmerizing. "Maybe even a bottle of scotch and a half-full glass. Someplace they thought they were coming back to but never did. Maybe someplace they were the morning before the police finally caught up with them. You know what I'm saying?"

Albert nodded. "I think I do."

"It probably sounds stupid, doesn't it?"

"Not at all." It was the truth. There was something

very sweet in her ability to imagine such a thing. It was far fetched as all hell, of course. To begin with, somebody sent them the map to get them here. Why would they pass the credit for such an incredible discovery to them? But there was no doubt in his mind that such a place could exist. A mobster gunned down in a police standoff would undoubtedly leave many secrets untold, but for something like that to exist here of all places...

But then again, why not?

"But you don't have any idea at all what you want to find?"

"I guess not. I mean, it's not so much *what* we find as that we find something at all, you know? It's like the way I wanted to solve the puzzles on the box. It wasn't what I expected to find, it was that I *could* find it."

He stood there a moment, considering what he'd just said. "For me, it's not really where I'm going as how I get there. Does that sound lame?"

Brandy smiled. "No. Not at all. I think maybe you've just got your priorities straight."

Albert shrugged. "I guess I'm not really all that

imaginative. I tend to look at the world logically. Mathematically, I guess."

"I don't know. I think it takes a good amount of imagination to solve puzzles like you do."

"Maybe. I don't know."

They began to walk again.

After a moment Albert said, "I think I'd value knowledge more than treasure. I'd love to uncover a secret."

Brandy smiled. "Like an eighty-year-old gangster hideout?"

Albert laughed. "Yeah. Just like that."

They continued forward and soon they were distracted by a loud buzzing noise from somewhere ahead. Albert recognized the sound at once. Flies. Lots of them. A tunnel branched off to the right ahead of them and the noise intensified as they approached it.

"Tell me we're not going that way."

Albert looked down at the map. "No. We go straight."

"Good."

As they passed, Albert caught a brief, overwhelming

whiff of decomposing flesh. *Rat*, he thought, pushing forward. Rats lived in places like these and they must die somewhere. But once the tunnel was behind him and the buzzing noise was fading, he wondered if he should have stopped to check the carcass. He remembered what Brandy told him the other day about students disappearing over the years. *They could have received a mysterious box, too.* Her words were humbling at the time and now he found them chilling. Suddenly it was far too easy to imagine that the rotting, maggot-ridden thing he left unseen in the darkness was a human corpse. What if she had been right about the sender of the box having malicious intentions and he just missed their only warning?

That's stupid. And yet, there was no stupidity in being cautious. They still didn't know who sent them the box and key.

But it was too late now. If he turned back he would have to voice his irrational thoughts and that would only serve to frighten Brandy.

But Brandy was already frightened. This place was far creepier than she imagined it would be. She reached into her purse and pulled out her cell phone. "No signal," she said after staring at the screen for a moment.

"Lot of concrete and rock between us and the tower, I'd imagine."

"Yeah." She put it back in her purse without turning it off. The idea that she could no longer phone for help made her uneasy.

Ahead of them, the tunnel opened onto another one. The map said they would turn right here and then take the next left after that. Then they'd be nearing the end. There weren't very many passages left on the map.

But it wasn't quite that easy. Although the passage they were now approaching was large enough to walk comfortably in, even side-by-side if they wished—the first of its kind in a while—its floor lay beneath four inches of standing water.

For a moment, the two of them stood in silence. They did not need to speak. They were both thinking the same thoughts. The imagination held no end to the things that could be in that stagnant and trash-littered water, from human filth and garbage juice to dead rats and live snakes.

Albert stepped up to the water's edge and shined his flashlight into the darkness ahead.

"I'm…" Brandy's voice failed her. There were no words to describe the disgust she felt at the thought of what she knew Albert was thinking. "No. I'm not wading through that."

"Maybe it's just rainwater."

"And maybe it's not."

The water was murky, but he could see the bottom. It was spotted with garbage, dead leaves and cigarette butts and a shimmering, oily film covered the surface. There was no current. He peered as far as his light would reach in both directions and then, satisfied that there were no bloodthirsty crocodiles waiting to snap off his legs, he stepped out into the water.

"Oh, gross!"

There was an icy sting to the water, and a smell wafted up from beneath him, like an old damp cellar, but with a subtle yet unmistakable swampy stench. "It's okay. It's only runoff from the street."

Brandy made a sound that was more a growl than a response.

"Come on. It's not that bad."

"I'm not getting my shoes in that."

Albert felt a pang of impatience. He understood that it was not an entirely pleasant idea, but he could certainly think of much worse situations than having to wade through dirty water. "So take them off."

"No way!"

They stood there, staring at each other. Albert saw the cobwebs on her shirt and in her hair and felt his impatience drain away as quickly as it came. He was eager to reach the destination on the map. His curiosity was driving him. He hadn't really been aware of what she must be feeling. He opened his mouth to apologize, but she didn't give him the chance. With a frustrated groan, she stepped off into the water. Her face twisted into an expression of pure disgust as it spilled over her heels and soaked into her socks.

Albert stood there a moment, watching her. He suddenly felt very bad.

"Well come on!" she snapped when he didn't move, and he turned quickly to lead the way. He still wanted to apologize, but he sensed it would do no good.

They waded on, their flashlight beams reflecting off the rippling surface of the water, making the moldy concrete walls shimmer. The next turn was about twenty feet down the tunnel, and the small but dry passageway that awaited them was a welcome sight.

"That was horrible."

"It was just drainage."

"I don't care."

"I'm sorry."

Brandy shook her head. "Forget it." In the end, it was her decision to follow him. It wasn't his fault that the passage was flooded. "Are we almost there yet?"

"I think we are." *Assuming these next few tunnels aren't twenty miles long*, he thought but didn't say. The map so far was accurate, but by no means to scale.

The next tunnel turned out to be only a few yards ahead and was extremely small, forcing them to continue once again on their hands and knees. It was too short for Albert to crawl through while wearing his backpack, so he removed it and pushed it ahead of him. At the very least it made a good tool for clearing out the cobwebs, although there seemed to be far less of them down here than there were in earlier tunnels.

Albert wondered what purpose a tunnel this small actually served. Was it some kind of overflow pipe? If water periodically filled this passage, it might explain the fewer spiders.

"We make a left up here somewhere."

About thirty feet into the tunnel, a hole had been knocked into the wall on the left and a larger tunnel, set lower than the one they were currently crawling through, was visible beyond.

"I think we're getting closer," said Albert as he examined the new tunnel. This one was older than all the rest. Its walls were made of rough stone, the ceiling rounded. The floor was packed earth. But it was tall enough to walk upright. There was a pile of rock and dirt leading down to the floor, as though the newer tunnel had been built right through the older one.

Albert shoved his backpack through the hole and then crawled out after it, carefully maneuvering himself across the rocks. When he was clear, he turned and offered Brandy his hand.

"Oh wow."

"Yeah."

"Do you think this is one of those tunnels I was talking about earlier? The really old ones?"

"I don't know. Sure *looks* ancient."

"Wow." She looked back at the hole through which they'd just crawled. The previous tunnel was actually a hollow cylinder of concrete protruding from the rubble. "Looks like they just built right over the top of it, doesn't it? What do you think it was used for?"

"Without knowing exactly how old it is, I don't think there's any way to know."

"Do you think it really predates the city?"

Albert considered it. The construction was definitely very rough. The surfaces were all uneven. It could have been built by anyone at any time. It certainly lacked the modern engineering of the newer, concrete tunnels, but that didn't necessarily mean much. The ability to dig a successful tunnel in the first place suggested some level of modern technological understanding. Didn't it? "I don't think so," he said at last. "I wonder if it would have survived the New Madrid earthquake."

Brandy thought about it for a moment while she lit

another cigarette. "I don't know. It could have."

Albert contemplated it for a moment. The New Madrid earthquake was one of the largest ever recorded in the United States. It was felt across over a million square miles. He wondered if such earthquake damage could account for the confusing labyrinth of tunnels. He supposed it was likely that some of the tunnels would have needed to be rerouted. But then again, hardly any disaster ever leveled *everything* man-made. There was a very good chance that this tunnel survived that quake. For all he knew, the rubble through which that last tunnel was laid was from an earthquake-induced cave-in.

"I guess there's no way to know."

"Maybe." Albert paused and looked at the map again. "Or maybe the answer to this will tell us."

"That would be cool." She leaned in to take a look at the map and let out a smoky breath that danced across Albert's face. She quickly waved it away, remembering that he did not smoke. "I'm sorry."

"It's okay," Albert said. "My mom smokes. I'm used to it. Bugs the hell out of my sister though."

"You have a sister?" she asked as they started

walking again.

"Yeah. Rebecca."

"Older or younger?"

"Older. She's twenty-five."

"Did she go to school here, too?"

"No. She went to UMSL," he replied, pronouncing the university by its acronym.

Brandy nodded. "I have some friends who go there. Why did you decide to come down here?"

"I guess I was looking for a reason to escape," replied Albert. "Most of the people I went to high school with found colleges in the St. Louis area. I wanted something different."

"Did you not have a lot of friends?"

"No, I had friends. A few, anyway." But not very many. He supposed it was a pretty lonely existence where he grew up. It was not as though his family didn't love him. He was close to his parents and he certainly had no quarrels with Becky, although when he was a boy he'd been the very epitome of the annoying younger brother. But he'd always had his space and they theirs and those spaces had always been respected. He spent most of his time with books and games. He didn't have the vast number of friends that Becky had, and he didn't have any interest in the sorts of activities that would have allowed him to make more. He also lacked the outgoingness of his sister, the cheerleader and homecoming queen. "How about you?" he asked. "Any brothers or sisters?"

Brandy shook her head. "I'm an only child. Daddy's spoiled little girl."

"I'll bet you have him wrapped around your little finger."

"Only a little bit."

Ahead of them, the tunnel forked off. One branch sank into the darkness to the left, the other to the right. "That's the last turn on the map. We go left."

Brandy turned and shined the flashlight back the way they'd come. "Did you hear something?"

Albert turned and studied the tunnel. "No. Did you?"

"I don't know. Probably not. I'm just paranoid."

"Come on."

They began to move again. They were getting close. Whatever it was the map was leading them toward—if it was leading anywhere at all—was at the end of that last tunnel. If there were any ill intentions involved in getting them down here they would soon find out.

"What do you suppose is down the right tunnel?"

"Probably closed off just like it was back there. Or caved in."

They turned at the fork and started down what the map suggested was the last leg of their trip. They walked in silence, their conversation having died away completely. Every now and then one of them would glance back the way they came. Somehow the seed of paranoia had been planted and now they were overrun with it.

Albert looked again at Brandy. It seemed surreal to him that she was actually here. A week ago he could only have fantasized about spending an evening alone with her. Again he wondered what it was that made her decide to come with him. Was it really just the adventure of it all? He couldn't help but hope that her decision was at least a little bit about him.

He turned forward again just in time to see a wall materialize out of the gloom. The two of them stopped and stared. It was a dead end.

"What the *fuck*?" Brandy turned and scanned the tunnel walls with her flashlight, trying to understand. They followed the map step by step, never faltering, they'd even waded that nasty, stagnant water, and for what? A dead end? She stared back the way they'd come, feeling like a rat in a maze with no solution. If whoever gave them the box and the key wanted them down here for sinister purposes, they were now literally up against a wall.

Albert walked closer to the wall. Something didn't look right.

"What now?"

He didn't reply. He was staring at this new wall. There was something about it.

"Did we take a wrong turn?"

"I don't know."

"Maybe we weren't supposed to go down this tunnel. Maybe this tunnel wasn't open when the map was drawn." Her voice was beginning to rise, fear sliding up her throat in great, wet, slithering clumps. All those stories that scared the hell out of her when she was a girl, those stupid stories about the haunted tunnels and the old witches with rotting flesh and appetites for children began to rise from the forgotten depths of her memory. *They eat you alive,* one of her friends told her years ago when she was just a child. *They eat you alive so you can feel every bite!*

"I don't think so." Albert reached out and touched the wall. He ran his fingers down it, feeling the rough texture of the stone. It was different from the surrounding walls somehow. He pressed his palm against the cold stone and pushed. The stones tumbled out of the wall with surprisingly little effort and their dead-end collapsed into a pile at his feet.

Brandy stared at him in disbelief. "How did you know to do that?"

"Hell if I know." He peered into the room that was hidden behind the wall, his eyes widening with disbelief.

"A false wall," Brandy wondered. "A thousand people could have walked right up to that wall and just turned back. All these walls. All these tunnels. It would be like finding a glass of water in the ocean." She turned her eyes away from the fallen stones and fixed them on Albert. "But *you* knew it would fall down."

"I didn't know," Albert insisted. He did not look at her, did not hear the accusation in her voice. He was looking into the next room, the room beyond the map.

Brandy glanced over her shoulder again, quickly this time. She could not help but wonder how trustworthy this man really was. She didn't really know him, after all. She clutched her purse with her free hand, pulling it to her breast like a lifeboat. Now another thought entered her mind. She could too easily imagine him turning on her down here, far below the streets of the Hill, where no one could hear her, and raping her, torturing her, murdering her. Down here he could take his time if he wanted. He could make her suffer for days. A chill ran through her as she imagined him turning to face her with the rotten, grinning face of the witch from her childhood nightmares.

Albert leaned into the hole he'd made, his head disappearing into the next room and another thought crossed her mind instead. Something would be in there, something dead and evil. It would lunge out and drag Albert into the darkness, tearing chunks out of him with its rotten teeth, *eating him alive.*

Suddenly, she did not know which scenario would be worse. Still clutching her purse, she took a step toward him, unable to ignore the shiver that was slowly creeping up her back. "See anything?"

He stepped into the next room and Brandy followed. What she saw next made her forget the horrors she was imagining.

Chapter 8

The room was ten feet across and eight feet deep. Its walls, floor and ceiling were all gray stone. There were no light fixtures. There were no doors or windows, only the opening through which Albert and Brandy entered and two smaller openings on the opposite wall. Five strange statues stood in this room, all of them apparently carved from the same gray stone from which the room itself was built.

Four of these statues were identical. Two stood flanking the entrance where Albert knocked down the false wall. The other two stood at the center of each of the two shorter walls on each side of the room. Each was a very vivid depiction of a naked and grossly disproportioned man. They were nearly eight feet tall and morbidly skinny, with taught flesh stretched over their long bones.

They had enormous Adam's apples and shockingly long penises that hung limp against their thighs. Their feet and hands were likewise deformed, their fingers and toes much longer than their proportions should have allowed. Their middle fingers were almost as long as Albert's forearm. They stood straight and stiff, backs to the wall, hands to their sides, feet together like sentinels at watch.

Directly in front of them, between the two openings in the facing wall, was the fifth statue. This was again the same elongated and faceless man, again carved from the same gray stone, but unlike the others, this statue was not standing upright and at attention. This one was frozen in motion, seemingly in the process of falling to his knees, hands lifted to what would have been his face, long fingers spread grotesquely in the air. There was something peculiar about the pose it was caught in, not precisely a pose that someone would depict in a statue. It was too random, too spontaneous, too *real*. It was like a photograph taken candidly in the middle of an action, the kind that never looked right because everything was frozen in transition. This man (or whatever it was) could have been collapsing in a furious fit of agony or in violent throes of joy. Without a face it was impossible to tell.

Somehow, Albert thought that was precisely the point of the statue. A life-sized and three-dimensional picture of the choice they needed to make.

"Holy shit!" Brandy was standing in front of one of the statues, her flashlight aimed at its enormous penis.

"Yeah, they're pretty messed up." But he'd already moved beyond the statues. There were no cobwebs in this room, he saw. The stone was free of dust, immaculately clean. He glanced back out into the tunnel from which they just entered. There were cobwebs out there, but not many. How recently had that tunnel been used, he wondered.

He turned his attention to the openings on the opposite side of the room, shining his flashlight into one and then the other. They were identical. Both dropped about six feet to a narrow tunnel that continued forward into darkness.

"They're so real," Brandy went on. "You can see every wrinkle and vein. They even have fingerprints. It's creepy." She backed away from the statue, as though she expected it to suddenly step forward and grab her. "Who do you think made them?"

"No idea." Albert was still studying the two passages. His eyes kept returning to the statue between the doors. *What do you know?* he wondered.

"What are they doing at the end of a closed up tunnel underneath Briar Hills of all places?"

"Don't know."

"It doesn't make any sense." An idea struck her then. "Hey, do you think we're in some kind of basement? Looks kind of like a museum of some kind."

Albert thought she was right. It did look like a museum of some kind. But he had never seen anything like these statues before. Besides, to his knowledge Briar Hills didn't have a museum with anything more interesting than antique tractors. And what kind of basement would have a room with an entrance like this? There was nothing practical about these passages at all.

Also, what kind of museum didn't have any apparent lighting or climate control?

Brandy walked over and shined her flashlight into one of the passages Albert was studying. "What now?"

Albert shook his head. He didn't know. "It's one or the other."

"So, what? Do we just try one?"

"I don't know. I don't think so." He had serious doubts about just dropping into one. He could not shake the feeling that the statue's unusual pose warned them of that, but he did not want to alarm Brandy any more than necessary.

"What does the map say?"

"The map stopped where we came through that wall."

"So how do we know which way to go?"

Albert shook his head again.

"Maybe they go to the same place."

"I doubt it." Albert was looking from one passage to the other, his head and the flashlight slowly turning from left to right, comparing them. Like with the wall, there was something that escaped him, something he was missing.

He took a closer look at the falling statue, studied it. It was tilted slightly to the right in its falling, but that meant nothing to him. His eyes fell on its right hand and he realized that its third finger was broken. He leaned closer and examined the shortened digit's stump. The stone there was flat and coarse, not smooth. The finger had definitely been broken from the statue, rather than carved this way. But where was it? He swept the floor with his flashlight, checking every corner and around the feet of each statue, but it was not there. He then shined his light down into the tunnel nearest the incomplete hand. There, right next to the wall, was a gray finger, complete with silky-smooth nail.

He dropped into the tunnel, paused long enough to peer ahead, and then scooped up the finger and climbed back up to where Brandy waited.

"What is it?"

"Finger," Albert replied. He examined it, puzzled, and then held it up to the statue's hand. As he'd thought, it didn't quite fit. There was another piece missing. But where was it? He didn't see it when he picked up the first piece. He walked to the other passage and shined his light into it, but there was nothing there, either.

"If it's so important to go the right way, why did the map stop back there?"

Albert thought about the box that led them here and suddenly he understood. "Maybe it didn't."

Brandy looked at him, curious.

He tucked the flashlight into his armpit and opened the box. He stirred through the contents for a moment and withdrew the small stone. He held it to the piece he'd found in the left tunnel and found a perfect fit. "Bingo." He reached up and held both pieces to the stump on the statue's right hand, completing it. "The game board."

"What?"

"The things in the box. I started thinking they were all pieces to a puzzle. If I could just solve the puzzle, I'd understand what it all meant. But I couldn't figure out how they all fit together. Now I realize my mistake. I was missing a place to put all the pieces of the puzzle. A game board. That's what this place is. It's one big game board." He shined his flashlight into the left tunnel, the one both nearest to the statue's broken hand and where he'd found the missing piece. "We go this way."

He looked into the tunnel he'd just pointed out and wondered. Did someone break off that finger intentionally? As impressive as these statues were, that seemed awfully rash. Wasn't there a better way to lead them through than by defacing these...whatever they were? But then again, he didn't know what the value of these things might be, and even less idea what the value might be to whoever sent them the box.

"Well," Albert said, a little nervous. "Let's get moving. Should I go first?"

"Yeah."

He slipped the stone back into the box, along with the other piece of the dismembered digit, and then slipped the box into the backpack. He also took the paint can from Brandy and dropped it into the bag. Finally, he slung the backpack over his shoulders, dropped into the hole and shined his flashlight into the next passage, chasing away the shadows. "Okay. Come on down."

Brandy hesitated for just a moment, wondering about his ability to solve these strange puzzles, almost without thinking, almost as though he already knew the way. A part of her wanted to turn and run, to just leave him here and get the hell out while she still could, but she was afraid to go back alone. She was also admittedly curious about where this strange place would lead them. With doubt gnawing at her mind, she followed Albert deeper still into the darkness.

Chapter 9

This next tunnel was too short to allow them to walk upright, but it was not as long as many of the similar passages they'd already traveled. It quickly opened into a large chamber at least twenty feet wide and high. This room was made of the same smooth, dark stone that the first room was built from, and was far too long for the flashlights to penetrate to the other end.

Along the walls, more of those strange, faceless statues stood like guards.

"Wow," marveled Brandy.

Albert nodded in agreement. Their flashlights could pick up three pairs of the faceless sentinels, but no farther, and the darkness beyond was disturbing to him.

He felt that something was there, lying silently in the shadows, waiting for them, perhaps watching them.

"Somebody was sure proud of these guys." Brandy was running her flashlight over one of the statues.

Albert was studying those up ahead. He didn't quite grasp it yet, but there was something strange about them. They were not all the same.

He took several steps into the room, his eyes moving from one statue to another, trying to understand what he was seeing. They really were like sentinels, diligently watching, guarding these weird chambers for reasons he could not imagine. As he walked deeper into the room, he found himself remembering what Brandy told him about some of the tunnels being older than the city, carved out of the earth in ancient times, and he shuddered at the thought of standing in such a timeless place.

The fourth pair appeared from the gloom and he realized exactly what it was that was different about each of them. He stopped and swept his light across the four on his left, then on his right, reassuring himself that he was, indeed, seeing the strange scene he now perceived. With each pair of statues, a single thing changed. They stood in the same position, hands at their sides, feet together, rigid, alert, but as they moved farther into the room, each pair of sentinels was…as odd as it seemed… slightly more *aroused* than the one before it. Their massive penises were actually growing progressively stiffer the deeper into the room they went.

"Somebody has a really sick sense of humor," Brandy said, but there seemed to be more anxiety in her voice than disgust.

"They definitely had an infatuation with the male body." Albert continued to walk, amazed at how the statues continued to appear, one pair after another, each more obscene than the last, but only marginally. The subtleness of the change between each sentinel was so slight that it was difficult to see, but as they appeared one by one from the darkness, it was too easy to imagine the stone organs becoming engorged with blood, almost as if it was his and Brandy's very presence that excited them. His eyes were drawn forward as he walked and he wondered what they would find at the end, when these stone sentinels were no longer mildly amorous but outright horny and wielding full-sized boners.

Perhaps Brandy wondered the same thing, because just then her cold hand slipped into his and squeezed.

"You mind?"

"No. Of course not."

She gave him a smile and then turned and examined the sentinels. "This place is so freaky. I hate how dark it is."

"I know. There's no lighting at all. No fixtures. No switches."

"Maybe it predates electricity."

"I wouldn't be surprised. But there aren't even places to hang torches. It's almost like this place was meant to remain in the dark."

"That's really creepy," Brandy replied, squeezing his hand a little harder.

Albert glanced at her. He didn't mean to keep scaring her. "I know."

On either side of them, the statues stood. Somehow, their blank faces made it easier to imagine that they were watching them.

"It's all just so weird," Brandy said.

"It is. It looks like the set for an X-rated Indiana

Jones movie."

Brandy laughed. "It does, doesn't it?"

"Yeah. All you need is a giant boulder shaped like a woman's breast rolling down the middle of the room."

Again Brandy laughed, and it gave them both courage. It was hard to be afraid of something that made you laugh.

"Indiana Jones and the Temple of the Happy Sentinels," Albert said, and Brandy laughed so heartily that she had to stop and wipe away tears.

Up ahead another pair of sentinels appeared. Albert had lost count by now, but their penises hovered in front of them, almost parallel with the floor.

"That's too funny."

Albert smiled. He was glad she was laughing. It made him feel better to know that she felt better.

Brandy tugged at his hand and led him to the nearest statue. "I can't believe how realistic they are, even for being all out of proportion." She ran her fingertips down the chest and stomach of the statue, admiring the craftsmanship of the sculpture. "Who do you think put them here?"

"Don't know." He was studying the statue's face, that blank, empty void that was all the artist had allowed them of human expression. Even blind, deaf and mute, it retained a strange illusion of wisdom and understanding. In its own faceless way it seemed to be contemplating something, perhaps its own sexuality, with a deepness that was nearly frightening, but that was more his imagination than anything he saw on the smooth, empty curve that was its face.

"What purpose do they serve?"

"Maybe none. Maybe no more purpose than a painting on a wall. Just a decoration. Or maybe they're as important to whoever made them as the cross or a sculpture of Jesus. Or maybe they were to help somebody navigate these corridors." He shrugged. "Who knows? Maybe they serve a very important purpose that we can't possibly imagine."

Brandy touched the smooth surface of the sentinel's groin, just above the penis, her fingertips sliding over it gracefully, delicately. They had no hair at all. "So realistic," she observed. She slid her hand down, below the penis to the testicles, which dangled like two heavy plums in their stone pouch. With the tip of her index finger, she followed the folds and wrinkles of its anatomy. It seemed as though it should give to her touch, folding and lifting like real flesh, but it was only stone. At last she lifted her hand to the penis itself. With her thumb and her fore and middle fingers, she softly grasped the giant member and traced its arc all the way to its tip, feeling the wrinkles and the veins as her fingertips slid along its cold, hard flesh.

Albert felt a nervous knot form in his chest as he watched her. There was something terribly erotic about the way she touched the statue. Though only stone, it seemed that it defied all laws of nature by not becoming instantly and fully erect at her sensuous touch.

"They're uncircumcised," Brandy observed as she traced the end of the stone foreskin with the tip of her middle finger. "Makes them look kind of uncivilized." She took her hand away from the statue's genitals and wiped it on her jeans as though she expected it to be dirty. "No. 'Uncivilized' is the wrong word. Primitive, maybe, or...I don't know. I'm not good with words. I mean if they were circumcised, they would seem more modern to me. If these things were really, really old, they might not have invented circumcision yet. Do you get what I'm trying to say?" She turned and looked at Albert, wanting to know if he understood what she was trying so awkwardly to say, but he was staring back the way they'd come, his flashlight fixed on the darkness behind them. "Albert?" She aimed her flashlight in the same direction, trying to see what he was looking at. "Something wrong?"

"No." But he wasn't sure. For just an instant he thought he'd seen something, a shadow moving in the dark, and perhaps a soft shuffling noise, but now it was gone, perhaps imagined. "Nothing wrong." He turned to her, gave her a reassuring smile and softly squeezed her hand. "Let's keep going."

From the darkness came more pairs of statues, their penises growing more and more erect, now pointing more up than down, but Albert became more aware of the darkness *between* the statues, the thick emptiness that their flashlights were so slowly washing away. There was something there, something in that darkness, something larger than the statues and far more profound.

The final pair of sentinels appeared, sporting full erections nearly as long as baseball bats, and in the darkness between them, shapes began to emerge. Albert took one more step and all those shapes leapt together. His heart skipped a beat with fright and he nearly cried out as a giant face appeared before him.

Brandy uttered a single, four-letter input and stared, amazed. Before them stood the enormous stone face of a woman, carved from the very stone like everything else in this incredible place. Its details were every bit as vivid as those of the sentinel statues. The expression was one of pure ecstasy, as though the woman were in the throes of some great orgasm, so intense that even looking at it seemed to trouble their senses and fill them with a strange sort of arousal. There were pores in her skin, and a faint blemish high on one cheek. Her eyes shimmered, appearing almost to contain real tears. She even had eyelashes, delicate and fine. Her mouth was wide open in a frozen scream of lust, her lips soft, her teeth slightly crooked. Her tongue was rough with taste buds, but with that same, strangely wet texture as her eyes. Her mouth was a door, opening into the wall and the next room.

Beyond her tonsils was utter darkness.

"Amazing," said Albert.

"Yeah. Is she what's got these boys so excited?"

"Maybe. I don't know what it means."

"She's so real."

"I know." He shined the flashlight over the surface of the face, studying it, and then peered into the gaping mouth. "There's something on the other side. Come on."

The two of them stepped into the screaming woman's mouth, careful of the teeth and the lips below and above them, half expecting it to snap closed and devour them both.

"Oh my god…"

It was Brandy who spoke. Albert was unable to even comment. They stepped out of the woman's throat and into another room, this one smaller, but still large enough that the light did not reach the other side. Directly in front of them, a stone woman stared back from the floor, her eyes wide, nearly bulging, her mouth open in a silent scream. She was naked, her back arched, her fingers clawing at the stone floor on which she lay, her legs spread wide apart, her feet in the air. A stone man, as human as the woman, complete with face and greedy, lustful expression, knelt between her spread legs, one hand closed around one of her ankles, the other groping for one of her breasts. They could have been real people, their skin soft and damp with sweat instead of hard, cold and smooth. Behind them, two men stood with a woman between them, all of them naked. One of the men was holding the woman, clutching her elbow in a painful grip with one hand while squeezing one of her breasts with the other. The other man held one of her legs up high while trying to guide his swollen penis into her. They might have been raping this woman but for the expression on her face, ferocious, greedy, uncontrollable in the storm of her lust, her free hand groping for the penis she so eagerly anticipated. Beyond them were more, dozens more, men and women, all of them as realistic as the stone face that led them into this room.

Albert took two steps forward, his flashlight sliding across the orgy of stone. He'd never seen anything like this, had not even imagined that something like this could ever have been created, not even in poor detail. Arms, legs, heads and other parts protruded from the walls all around them, as if this display continued beyond the perimeter of the room. Every imaginable type of sexual activity was depicted here. There were women and men giving and receiving oral sex with no apparent sexual preference. Others were masturbating themselves or others or both at once. Every sexual position he could possibly think up and a few he'd never imagined jumped out at him, life sized and three-dimensional.

His light gravitated toward the back of the room, where the orgy was intensified, and he went to it, almost unaware that he was moving. Directly in front of the door that stood on the other side was a pile of stone bodies, each one clawing and tearing, a violent and sexual brawl, where even in stone he could see scratches and bruises as perhaps fifty of these stone men and women fought for something he could not see, something above them, much higher than the ceiling would allow him to gaze upon.

Atop it all, a single woman rose up, buried to her hips in clawing, groping arms, covered in claw marks and bleeding from her lip and nose. Even one of her fingers seemed to have been broken in the scuffle. She was reaching up to the ceiling, her face contorted into such a deep yearning that Albert could hardly comprehend it in his own mind. Her eyes shined with want, her mouth open, silently crying out for whatever it was that lured her upward.

As he stared at this, Albert became aware of his own desires. His own penis was as hard as those around him, throbbing painfully against the front of his jeans. He was breathing hard, almost panting.

"Albert..."

He had almost forgotten about Brandy. He turned to find her standing just behind him, her eyes locked on that same, violent orgy. She was breathing in quick, shallow pants, her breasts rising and falling beneath her sweatshirt. Her knees were slightly bent as though she urgently needed to pee. With her free hand she rubbed at the crotch of her jeans as though coaxing a dull pain. The flashlight trembled, ready to fall. He went to her, meaning to steady her, but she flung her arms around him and kissed him with such ferocity that he was shoved backward against the motionless yet flailing stone foot of a woman who might have been choking to death on a man's entire, swollen penis and loving every agonizing second of it. He heard something strike the floor and was barely aware through his confusion that it was Brandy's flashlight.

The pain in his back was no match for the one in his head. It was like his brain was rotating inside his skull. The things he saw made his eyes ache and his genitals throb. His yearnings were more than he could bear. In moments he and Brandy stripped each other bare and were writhing on the floor, caught in the same sort of furious sex that the stone statues depicted all around them. The world spun and the statues twirled with it, the pornographic images bombarding them as they did what no one on earth could possibly describe as making love, for it was pure animal lust without romance or even a preference for who their partner was, as long as that partner could satisfy that endless burning within.

They did it not just once, but continuously. With each orgasm, Albert was maddeningly unsatisfied and bursting with fierce wanting for the next. He kept thrusting, willing his softening body to respond, forcing himself to do it over and over again, long after his body began to ache with the exertion. He was barely aware of the object of his lust. She cried out with her own hungry wanting and met his violent thrusting, clawing at him, begging him not to stop, even when each heavy thrust began to drive nails of pain deep into her body. Their voices rose into the echoing darkness as they were both raped by the strange, overwhelming lust that somehow emanated from this gray room of stone perversions. At some point Albert kicked a statue and felt an icy wave of pain wash up his foot, but he barely noticed it. At some point Brandy ripped out a lock of his hair, but he barely felt that, too. And at some point he was vaguely aware that one of the statues was moving among the others, but that did not matter any more than the pain. All that mattered was the lust.

Gradually the light receded and darkness swallowed them. And as the light fell, so did the fires within them. With one final, quaking orgasm, they both collapsed in utter exhaustion on the cold floor, hardly more than sweat-slicked piles of naked and quivering flesh, and slipped into weary sleep.

Chapter 10

As he awoke, Albert was first aware of the darkness. It baffled him, confused him the same way that the cold feel of the hard floor under him and the chilly air on his damp skin confused him. For a moment he could not remember where he was, but his memories swam back to him as surely as did consciousness. He remembered Brandy and the room with the stone orgy and the thing they'd done together as though the very sight of those statues was enough to fling them into furious, sexual wanting. He remembered the sex and the confusion. He remembered something else, too, something he'd seen while in the throes of an orgasm that wouldn't satisfy him: a shadowy shape moving among the statues.

Suddenly it dawned on him that it was dark and terror burst from every fiber of his being.

He scrambled to his feet and then stood there, naked and shivering, listening to the darkness, trying to hear the breathing of an invisible intruder. But there was not a sound but his and Brandy's breathing and the thudding of his own heart. The silence was as eerie as the darkness, but it was also comforting. They were at least alone. He thought about waking Brandy, but he knew that if he could find the flashlights first, then she might be less afraid when she awoke. He turned, trying to find his bearings, and a piece of stone struck him in the corner of his eye, sending a flash of pain through his already throbbing head.

He cursed and stumbled away, only to be jabbed in the back by something else. Solid stone statues surrounded him. Although they looked as soft as real flesh, they were definitely not. He stopped and stood for a moment, wondering what to do, and as he blinked away tears of pain from his stinging eye he became aware that he could see, although only barely. There was a dim glow from beyond the next door.

He made his way toward the light, feeling around the statues with his arms held up in front of his face, waiting for another rogue limb to jab him, perhaps putting out an eye way down here in the darkness. As he crept through the crowded stone orgy, he found that he could see the outline of the doorway. The light was slightly brighter in the next room.

Rectangular, about ten feet across by fifteen feet wide, this next room was empty. The intruder wasn't here. Neither were there any statues, pornographic or otherwise. He could make out two corridors. One was on the far right side of the opposite wall, leading forward. The other led left from the far corner. The light was coming from this direction.

Quickly, and without looking back, he moved toward the lighted corridor and peered down it. About twelve feet into the passage another corridor branched off to the right. About four feet beyond that was a sharp right turn. There, at that right turn, the light was brighter still.

He began to walk toward the light, desperate to get his flashlight back, but as he approached the first passage, his bare foot struck something and he froze. Around him, the tunnel was filled with the soft sound of light metal skidding across smooth stone. For a moment he stood there, unable to move, certain that something dark and malicious must have heard the noise and would soon come rushing toward him. But no such horror could be seen.

After a moment, he let go his held breath and began forward again. He bent and picked up the object he'd kicked, puzzled. How did Brandy's glasses get way out here?

Same way the flashlight left the room.

He glanced back over his shoulder at the room he was leaving behind. He hoped Brandy would be safe until he returned. He didn't realize the light was so far away. Perhaps he shouldn't have left her alone, but it was too late now. He might as well get the flashlight first.

He crept on, his bare body shivering with fearful anticipation. He wished he could see better than he could, but with each step his vision improved. He peered up the first corridor as he passed, but could see only darkness. His flesh tingled with fear. He could too easily imagine someone standing in that darkness, watching him, calculating his movements, waiting for his guard to drop.

He made the turn at the end of the corridor and gazed ahead. The tunnel went on out of sight into the darkness. About twenty feet ahead, the tunnel branched to the left. The light was strong there, but there was something ominous about the darkness beyond that turn.

What the hell was he thinking coming down here? He'd actually been willing to come here alone! What would have happened then? What would have become of him? He hurried on, trembling with anxiousness, bracing himself against whatever horror was certain to come charging out of that darkness beyond the light.

But nothing came after him. He turned left, into the light, and there was his flashlight. It was lying motionless on the ground. Beside it, another passage went right. Beyond it, about fifteen feet away, the corridor broke into a tee and went both left and right.

He rushed to the flashlight and snatched it off the ground. He half expected a trap, but he could no longer stand not having it in his hand.

He gazed up the tunnel to the right. There were no more passages to be seen in that direction for as far as the light would reach.

All these corridors… This was some kind of maze. And the flashlight seemed to be leading him toward *this* passage.

A part of him wanted badly to see where that passage led, despite the fear he felt, but he could do no such thing. He needed to get back to Brandy.

He made his way back to the previous passage, gave the tunnel to the left a brief glimpse with the flashlight and then continued back the way he'd come. He did not like this at all. The whole idea of not being alone gave him chills all the way to his soul. The fact that this presence managed to steal his flashlight intensified that chill until his whole body trembled with anxious anticipation.

"Albert?"

He heard her voice as he rounded the turn in the corridor. She'd awakened before he could return after all.

"*Albert? Where are you?*" There was panic in her voice, and he could hardly blame her. He should not have left her back there.

"I'm here, Brandy." He broke into a sprint and

hurried back to the room where he'd left her.

Brandy froze in the flashlight beam like a deer in headlights. She was on all fours, crawling around on the cold floor, searching for her clothes and her glasses and of course for him. She was still stark naked, her golden hair dangling around her startled face, her blue eyes wide and frightened, tears streaming down her cheeks. Beside her was the flashlight she'd been carrying. The lens was broken and it offered no light. Albert vaguely remembered the sound of it hitting the ground when she threw herself at him.

Not a stitch of their clothing could be seen.

"Albert?"

He was staring at her there amid the statues, her naked breasts accented by gravity, her nipples erect from the chill, her bare buttocks up in the air, her whole body covered in gooseflesh, and again he was stricken with that bizarre and fierce arousal, that animal lust.

He closed his eyes, squeezing them hard against the strange urges he felt, and in just a moment he felt himself calming. What the hell was wrong with him?

"Albert, is that you?"

Again he opened his eyes. Brandy was getting to her feet now, modestly covering her breasts but not that other part. That part of her was fair and golden, a small tuft of lovely blonde, a place forbidden to his eyes, but unlocked in a moment of strange lust. Suddenly he was aroused again, as stiff as the last pair of sentinels in the previous room.

He turned and bolted from the doorway, turning away from Brandy and the room entirely.

"*Albert!*" She began to cry again, utterly terrified, and Albert felt sick to have left her in the dark like that. *"Albert! Don't leave me!"*

"It's okay. I'm right here."

"*Come back!*"

"Come to me!"

"*Albert, please!*"

"I *can't!*" He growled with frustration. He wanted to go to her, but he couldn't, and he didn't even know why. "What the *fuck!*"

"Where are you?" She was getting closer now.

"I'm right outside the door." He shined the light at the door, not looking at it. "You can see the light, right?"

"Yeah. Sort of. But I can't see anything else. My glasses."

Albert looked down at her glasses. He was still holding them in his hand. "I've got your glasses. Come to me, okay Brandy?"

"Okay." She sounded pitiful. "I'm coming."

He could hear her footsteps. She was just inside the door, but moving slowly, likely feeling her way around the statues that had bruised him up a good deal on his way out.

At last she stepped through the doorway. Her arms were still crossed over her breasts, as though unaware that her bottom half was showing as well. She spotted Albert and flung herself into his arms. *"What the fuck is going on?"*

"I don't know." He held her that way for a long time, letting her weep against his bare shoulder, trying not to think that she was naked or about what they'd done together. He kept his ears open and watched both the doorway behind and the tunnels ahead, keeping an eye out for whoever or whatever had moved their stuff.

"Why did we do that?" Her words were nearly

inaudible, muffled against his shoulder and by her own sobs.

"I don't know. It was that room. Something about it."

Brandy pulled away from his embrace and covered herself again, this time covering all of her, useless as it was. "Where are my clothes?"

"I don't know. I didn't see them." He gave her back her glasses and she revealed her body long enough to slip them onto her face, both hands trembling so badly that he was afraid she might poke herself in the eye with one of the earpieces.

"Fucking *hell*!" She leaned back against the hard stone wall. "I couldn't control myself in there." She growled with a self-hatred that nearly broke Albert's heart.

"I'm sorry."

"*Good*," she spat. "You're sorry. *Wonderful*. Like that changes anything."

"I guess it doesn't." Albert turned and walked to the tunnel he had not taken before.

"Where are you going?"

"Just looking."

Albert stood with his back to her now. He was afraid he was going to cry and he did not want that. If it happened he certainly did not want her to see it. He could think of much worse things that could happen to them than a freak humping. Being mauled by whatever took their clothes was not last on that list. Nevertheless, he felt a deep shame at having lured her into such a thing, and an even deeper hurt at the thought that she may never forgive him for it.

There was no movement ahead of them in either of the tunnels. Everything was as he'd left it. Of course, whatever was in here with them probably possessed enough sense to stay well away from the light. In many of the passages they'd traveled, their flashlights did not nearly reach the other end. Anything could have stood right out in the open and watched their every move, completely unobserved.

"Where's our clothes?"

Albert wanted to lie, but there was no way around it. "I don't know. They're gone."

"How the fuck are they *gone*?"

"Somebody was in there with us while we were… whatever it was we were doing."

"We were *fucking*!" she spat. "God *damn* it! What *was* that place?"

"I don't know."

Brandy made a noise that was half whimper and half groan and cursed.

Without turning back to her, Albert said, "I saw something when we were…" he started to avoid it, but saw no point in it, "…fucking. I couldn't do anything. I was out of control."

"Yeah, no kidding."

Albert bit his lip and closed his eyes. After a moment, he went on. "When I woke up it was dark, I followed the light through that tunnel over there. I found your glasses just a little ways up and the flashlight was farther ahead."

"I didn't see anybody."

Albert turned and looked at her. She was sitting on the floor with her back to the wall now, hugging her knees in front of her and shivering. She was terrified and ashamed, he could see that in her face, but there was something else there as well, something much colder. "What?"

"I didn't see anybody. I woke up and you were gone."

He wanted to argue that logic, but he honestly could not. "I don't—"

"Why did you want me to come down here with you?" she asked, cutting him off.

Albert stared at her. He knew she didn't fully trust him, but now that he was under the gun, he could hardly believe it. "Because this is half yours," He replied cautiously. "It's your key."

But her cold eyes never left his.

"Do you think I could come up with something like that?" he asked suddenly, lifting a finger toward the doorway of the sex room. "I'm a fucking Computer Science major! Last I checked that didn't include fucking with people's heads!"

Brandy flinched with each word that he spoke. "I didn't say you made it," she said, her voice shakier than before.

Albert's anger was sudden and furious, but it melted

away as he saw the fear in her eyes. In a calmer voice he said, "You think I led you here on purpose."

She said nothing. She only stared at him with those same cold eyes she'd fixed on him in the second floor lounge of Lumey, except this time those eyes were wet with tears.

He backed up against the wall and closed his eyes. "I didn't know anything about this. If I had, I wouldn't have come like this. I'd... I don't know. I'd have found another way."

Brandy stared at him. None of this made any sense to her, but she did know that he was right. There was no way he could have made something like that. That didn't mean, however, that he hadn't discovered it before.

Albert sighed. "What do you want me to do?"

"What?"

"Tell me what you want me to do. I can't make you trust me. You have no reason to. I fucked up, probably ruined your life. I might as well have raped you. So it's your game now. What do you want me to do?"

Brandy stared at him and said nothing.

He held the flashlight out to her. "You want the

flashlight? You can be in charge. You can just go if you want, leave me here."

"Leave you here?"

"Yeah. Go ahead. Good luck getting back through that room, though. And as for these tunnels, from what I've seen they're a maze."

"What are you saying?"

"I don't know." He sat down against the wall opposite her and stared down at the floor. "I didn't do anything. I just did what the box told me. I solved the puzzle, that's all. I didn't know anything like this was going to happen or I wouldn't have. You were right. I should've just thrown the damn thing away."

Brandy lowered her eyes to the floor as well and remained silent.

Albert felt the silence drag on for nearly a minute before speaking again. "I *am* sorry. I couldn't control myself in there either, you know."

For a moment he did not think that she would reply, but then she did. "I know."

"Good."

"What do we do now?" she asked so softly he almost

didn't hear her.

"I guess we push on."

She looked up at him with fear in her eyes.

"I don't know about you, but I don't want to go back in that room."

Brandy lowered her eyes again and slowly nodded. She couldn't argue that. Besides, their clothes were missing. If he was telling the truth, he found her glasses and the flashlight up ahead. Maybe there'd be a trail to lead them to the rest of their things. Hopefully it wouldn't lead them to anything bad.

"There is someone in here with us," Albert said after a moment. "I swear to you it's not me. I didn't come here to hurt you and I won't let anything else hurt you. I think I've done enough damage already by talking you into coming with me in the first place."

"You didn't talk me into it," she said. "I came because I wanted to. It's like Grandma's basement. I never could resist the adventure."

"I'm really sorry."

"I know." She looked up at him with eyes that were now more hurt than hateful. "I want to believe you so bad. I need to believe you. If I can't, then that means I'm all alone down here."

Albert nodded. "You're not."

"But all I know is that *you* brought me the box, *you* figured it out, *you* solved all the puzzles and brought me here and... And when I woke up just now, you were gone and so were our clothes."

"Yeah, I guess that does look pretty bad for me."

"I thought for a minute that you'd just left me there."

"I'd never."

"But I thought you did. I couldn't think straight. My head hurt. *Everything* hurt." She glanced to the side as she said this, embarrassed, and Albert knew what she meant by that. His genitals hurt after the furious sex they'd shared. Her womanly parts probably hadn't fared much better. "I didn't think about the reasons," she went on. "I just knew that something strange happened and I was naked and alone."

"I meant to be back before you woke up."

Brandy said nothing.

"You can have the flashlight. I meant that. Yours broke when you dropped it. If it makes you feel better, keep it." He placed it on the floor and slid it over to where she sat. She grabbed it and clutched it against her. "If nothing else I guess you can club me with it if you feel like you have to."

Brandy gave him a humorless smile. "Maybe I will."

"Good."

"I'm scared."

"Me too. But remember, just because we're not alone doesn't mean we're in danger. Whoever it was had the opportunity to kill us both in there, but didn't."

"Maybe he's playing with us."

"Maybe."

"I'm not a virgin."

Albert looked up at her suddenly, shocked at this sudden confession. She was staring at the flashlight. He could still see the wet trails her tears had left upon her cheeks.

"I mean I wasn't before, you know." She looked at him now, her blue eyes shimmering. "Please don't think you took that from me. I gave that away when I was fifteen. I regret it, but I can live with it. Just like I can live with what we did in there just now."

For a moment Albert could only stare at her. She didn't hate him. That was what she was telling him. She did not hate him and, at least for the moment, she did not blame him. Whatever happened in there was no different than rape, but at least it hadn't robbed her of her first time. It was one small shred of comfort that she was allowed.

"I'm not a virgin," she said again, as much to herself as to him.

Albert looked down at his hands, not wanting to look into her eyes. "I was."

Brandy forgot the chill she felt. All of the tension that filled her body rolled off of her in an instant. She forgot about trying to hide herself. She stared at him as he sat there, his muscular legs bent only slightly, his belly softly folded by his posture, his shoulders slack. He looked very pale in the shadows. She suddenly felt very selfish. "I'm sorry."

But he shook his head. "Don't be. Strange or not—*intentional* or not—it was kind of nice. I mean, weird. But you know. Nice. I guess I'm glad it was someone like you. I honestly can't think of a nicer person to... You know… Randomly fuck." He could feel himself blushing now.

She forced a smile through her fear and anger. "You're nice." He was *too* nice. Suddenly she felt like such a bitch.

"I think the flashlight might have been pointing the way we're supposed to go up ahead," Albert said after a moment. "I think our clothes might have gone that way."

"And if not?"

"Then we're screwed. Whoever it was took my backpack and the box."

A sudden realization struck Brandy like a slap to the face. "Shit! And my purse!"

"Yeah. And my wallet." He stood up and turned to the passage on the left. "How about I lead and you follow with the light?"

Brandy stood up and wiped her face with the back of her hand. "Okay."

Chapter 11

Beyond the point where Albert found the flashlight, the corridor did not branch off. It went straight about a hundred yards into the darkness and then made a sudden left turn and went on for another forty yards before turning back to the right again. Albert walked several paces ahead of Brandy, squinting to see into the darkness. He wished he was still carrying the light, if only so that he didn't have to follow his own shadow through the gloom, but he'd promised Brandy she could have it and he meant it. He needed her to trust him. She'd said that without him she'd be alone and it was no different for him. But the limits of his courage were being tested. At every turn of the tunnel, he expected something to be there, something dark and sinister, something monstrous, something with teeth and claws and appetite and hate, but turn after turn there was nothing. Their progress remained unhindered, but their anxiety grew. He felt as though they were walking through a carnival funhouse and waiting for the next monster to leap out and startle them. He had to keep reminding himself to breathe.

After perhaps ten minutes, although it felt like hours, the tunnel made a sharp right and brought them face to face with a waiting figure.

Brandy screamed and stumbled backward, even as she recognized it as another of those faceless statues.

Albert too was startled, but more by Brandy's scream than by the sight of the sentinel. He gazed at it, taking in every detail. This statue was on its knees, the smooth surface that was its face turned up to the ceiling, its hands upturned and lifted as if in offering. From its long fingers hung his backpack and Brandy's purse.

"I'm sorry," said Brandy, meaning for the scream.

"It's okay," Albert assured her.

"What does it mean?"

Albert shook his head. "Good question." Behind the

statue, the tunnel continued on, but its floor began to slope downward, ever deeper into the earth at a shallow, but discernible angle.

"A peace offering, maybe?"

"Or a trap."

Albert stared at it. "I don't know. Seems too easy. After all, I'd call that *last* room a trap." He stepped toward it, beginning to reach for them.

"Be careful."

He was touched by her concern, even if it was only because she would be alone down here if something happened to him. "Stand back, okay?"

Stand back she did. When Albert looked again, she was standing all the way against the wall, her eyes wide with worry. She was clutching the flashlight nervously in front of her. She'd entirely stopped trying to hide herself by now, and he could see her breasts and the lovely tuft of soft, blonde hair where her torso vanished between her thighs. In the dark surroundings, her skin was like the moon in a dark sky, radiant, flawless, glowing gently in the gloom like a beacon. He could see gooseflesh on her arms, thighs and breasts from the coolness of the room, and her small nipples stood fully erect.

He saw that her expression had melted into one of puzzlement, and then realized that it was because he was staring.

He turned away from her and reached for their belongings.

"Be careful. Please."

Albert took the strap of the purse and one strap of the backpack and lifted. Nothing blew up. No lethal darts flew from concealed slots in the walls. No giant boulder —breast-shaped or otherwise—came rolling toward him. There was no poisonous gas, no flames, no spikes anywhere in sight. He was not crushed, maimed or decapitated. This wasn't Indiana Jones. This was something far different, far more real, and if he was going to die, it wasn't going to be now. He took the bags down and held the purse out to Brandy, who came toward him, her hand held out to take it and an expression of great relief adorning her face.

Nothing was missing. The box was still inside the backpack. Brandy's wallet was still in her purse, as were her keys and cell phone. After a quick inventory, Brandy confirmed that everything but their clothes had been returned.

Except that *Albert's* wallet and keys were still in his jeans.

Unable to do anything about it regardless, Albert dismissed his missing property for the time being and slipped the backpack onto his naked back. He then turned and studied the statue again.

Without the items dangling from its hands it looked less like a pose of godly offering than a pose of worship. And yet, what was there to worship in this empty corridor? He wished the damn things wore faces.

"Well," said Brandy, "we have our bags." She poked a cigarette into her mouth and lit it.

"Yeah, but not our clothes."

"Yeah. I feel so weird walking around like this."

"Me too."

"Do we keep going?"

Albert nodded. "I think we should."

He began to walk. Brandy drew the strap of her purse over one arm and her head and then followed, their combined wardrobe consisting entirely of a purse, a backpack, a pair of glasses and the jewelry they wore—two watches, four rings, a necklace and a pair of earrings between them. The two of them descended into the next tunnel, hand in hand, wielding a single flashlight between them.

Albert wondered how far they had traveled and if they were still under the Hill. He thought that they must be at least beyond the limits of the campus, and possibly even outside of the city, but they very well could be right back where they started, hundreds of feet beneath the entrance to the service tunnel. He wished there was some way of knowing just how far down they'd gone, how much rock and dirt was between the two of them and the world that knew sunlight.

Albert stopped before they had walked thirty feet. He almost didn't notice the subtle shift in the color and angle of the stone. The path ahead lay under water, and the surface was as still as a pane of glass.

Once more Brandy uttered her preferred four-letter word, but Albert barely heard her. He turned, suddenly very nervous, and looked back the way they'd come.

"What?"

"Whoever took our clothes didn't come this way."

"*What?*"

"That water's as still as ice. Nothing's disturbed it recently."

"Are you sure?" The fear in her voice was unmistakable. He wished he was better at keeping his concerns to himself. He was sure this would be much easier for her if she could just believe that they were alone down here. "How is that possible? The *bags*."

"Whoever it was," Albert explained, "must have come this way, dropped your glasses and the flashlight, then hung the bags and backtracked. Probably while we were still sleeping." Albert remembered fumbling around in the dark after he awoke in the sex room and wondered if whoever was doing this to them passed by him there and then, close enough to touch, but unseen in the darkness. The thought made him shiver.

Brandy squeezed his hand and drew close again. Another of those sick noises escaped her throat. He knew how she felt.

Albert stared back up the path, wishing he could see through the darkness. Then an idea struck him. "Stay here." Without waiting to see if she would actually stay, he jogged back up the tunnel, removing his backpack as he went.

But the thought of remaining behind and letting him run off into the darkness was unacceptable. She ran after him, desperate not to let him out of her reach. "Wait up!"

"I'm coming right back." But she wasn't listening. With Brandy on his heels, unwilling to be left alone, Albert ran back up the slope toward the praying statue. About halfway there he stopped and began to rifle through the backpack.

Brandy watched as he withdrew the paint can and removed the lid. He placed both on the floor, spacing them out so that they would be hard to miss in the darkness. She immediately understood his plan. Without a light, anybody following them would likely trip over one or the other, causing one or both of the objects to roll down the gentle slope to the water. The noise would alert them if they were still anywhere in the vicinity.

With one quick look back up the slope toward the statue, he grabbed Brandy's hand and hurried back to the still pool of water at the bottom of the tunnel.

"Can you go on?"

"Through the water?"

"Yeah."

The look on her face told him she didn't think so.

"Come on. I'll go first, but you have to stay close."

The mirrored surface shattered as Albert's foot struck the water and a shimmering ripple of reflected light instantly flooded the room. It was cold, probably the same temperature as the cool air that surrounded them, but upon their naked flesh it was hard to believe it could be so cold without freezing. Behind him, Brandy gasped, the cold as sudden as an electrical shock on her bare toes.

"So cold," she hissed, and Albert could hear the shiver in her voice.

"I know," he said. "Just be strong, okay?"

"Okay."

Albert had hoped that the water was only knee deep or so, but step by step it grew deeper and deeper as the floor sloped downward, slowly creeping up their sensitive thighs to the base of their buttocks, and mercilessly climbing the tender flesh of their lower backs and bellies. Violent shivers raced through them. Their teeth hammered together. Albert felt the weight change on his back as the backpack filled with water, growing lighter and lighter as more of its weight slipped beneath the surface.

As the water reached Brandy's armpits, she whimpered Albert's name, a pitiful, broken sound no louder than a whisper.

"I know," said Albert again, his voice no stronger than hers. "I know. Just a little farther."

The flashlight dipped beneath the water and their submerged bodies were illuminated by the glow. Albert could see nothing below the surface. No fish or frogs or snakes made their home here. It was pure and clean, which was certainly good, but the cold made it hard to relish such fortune.

The water slipped over their shoulders and they began to swim, their feet losing the welcome touch of the stone, and as they pushed farther, the ceiling drew down upon them. Albert prayed that the tunnel did not submerge completely.

The backpack, now fully soaked, again began to work against Albert, threatening to drag him down as he struggled forward. But he did not have time to think about it. At that moment, from somewhere in the darkness at their backs, came the clang and clatter of the paint can as it rolled down the slope of the tunnel. Albert's trap was sprung.

"Albert!" This time Brandy's voice was sharp and clear, tinged with a harsh edge of panic.

"Come on!" They swam on, struggling against their shivers. Behind them, the paint can continued its long chorus of clanging and clattering as it tumbled down to the water where it was finally silenced with a hollow splash.

Albert was suddenly thankful for their lack of clothes. It made swimming easier and he knew they would dry much more quickly without their jeans and shoes. But even with this going for them they'd be lucky to get out without catching pneumonia.

He could hear Brandy gasping and spitting behind him. It was hard to swim in water this cold. The shivering interfered with breathing, making each breath a struggle and therefore every stroke more laborious than the last.

Suddenly the flashlight fell dark and Albert's panic

was matched only by Brandy's terrified shriek. She gave it a violent shake and light again flooded the passage.

"It's okay," he assured her, but he knew the water wasn't good for the batteries. A battery-powered flashlight could shine for hours underwater, the charge merely spent faster, but it could possibly cause further blackouts like the one they just experienced, and they needed the light in this place.

It occurred to Albert that the ceiling was again retreating from their heads, and when he tried to touch bottom he found that he could. "Almost there," he told her. "It's getting shallower."

Brandy did not respond.

As the water withdrew from around their necks and past their shoulders to their chests, the air became like snow, chilling their dripping bodies until they were nearly numb with cold. As it sank down his thighs and walking became easier, Albert pulled Brandy forward and walked behind her, trying his best to warm her by rubbing her shoulders, knowing he was probably doing little to help, but trying anyway.

"Oh God," Brandy stuttered as she stepped onto dry

land, her arms wrapped around herself in a fierce hug, clutching the flashlight so tightly that her knuckles had gone white. "So cold."

Albert dropped the backpack and pulled her into his arms. Her skin was icy to the touch and he worried for her health. He did not know how close they were to hypothermia, and he'd already done enough to the poor girl just by bringing her to this twisted place.

"Freezing!"

"I know." He looked back at the water they'd just crossed, back into the darkness that shrouded the dangers beyond. The cold was bad, but he had a feeling it was far from the worst thing in these tunnels.

Chapter 12

"I'm sorry about your stuff."

Brandy shook her head. "Not your fault." She had dumped most of the contents of her purse onto the stone floor and was picking through them. Her cigarettes and lighter were both ruined, as was a small collection of gum, cough drops and breath mints. Much of her makeup was also among the casualties. But the worst was her cell phone, which was still on, was still glowing, but would probably be ruined long before it could dry. She shook some of the water off it and then turned it off. There was nothing she could do now.

"Do you have insurance on it?"

Brandy nodded. Thankfully she'd decided to pay the

extra couple of dollars a month for the protection plan just for such an emergency, but it was still a pain. She gathered her belongings back into her purse, salvageable and ruined alike, and began to rub her hands over her arms and shoulders. The chill was lessening, but it would not go away completely. The shivers remained, like unending aftershocks in the wake of a great earthquake. She was beginning to think she might never be warm again.

Albert closed and locked the box and put it back into his backpack. Its contents had remained dry throughout their frigid swim. "We should probably keep moving." They had been sitting there for almost fifteen minutes now, warming up as well as they could and listening for telltale splashes that would announce the approach of their mysterious pursuer. "It'll help us to stay warm if nothing else."

He stood up and shouldered his backpack. He hissed at the icy feel of its wet fabric against his naked back. Brandy stared up at him, her lovely eyes swimming over his naked body. She looked him up and down, actually *looking* at him for the first time since he lost his clothes, and she did not care that he saw her looking at him. Her eyes ultimately fell upon his privates. He was of a modest, but not unpleasing size, not big enough to have hurt her in the sex room, thankfully, but certainly large enough. She saw that he was circumcised, and that he had shriveled in the cold. She wondered what it would look like if he were hot instead of cold, and what it would look like fully erect. In the insane lust of the sex room, she had not actually seen him. In fact, she barely remembered any details at all. It was nothing more than a blur of insane and insatiable desire.

Albert felt uncomfortable. He watched her as she stared at him, her expression nearly empty, as though she were staring at some boring piece of art rather than at his personal anatomy. He wanted to turn away, to start walking up the slope and toward the unknown that lay ahead, just to get away from those eyes, but he could not. He was easily as fascinated by her looking at him as he was embarrassed by it. He wondered what she was thinking. With all that had happened down here, he couldn't imagine what she must be feeling. He could barely comprehend all the things *he* was feeling.

The truth of the matter was that she was hardly thinking anything at all. Her head still hurt. Her shivering had only worsened the throbbing pain that she awoke with in the sex room. More than anything she wanted to go home, to forget this hateful place and move on with her life. But at the center of all this was Albert, and she still did not know what to think of him. Somewhere deep down, she believed—or maybe just *wanted* to believe— that he was as much a victim of that horrible room as she was, but she still didn't know him.

At last she shifted her eyes to his, her face still empty of any perceptible emotion, and nodded. She was ready. She stood up and slid the strap of her purse over her head and arm, still shivering.

They stood for a moment, looking at each other with their teeth chattering and their skin covered with gooseflesh. Albert wanted to speak, but all of the words that came to him were inadequate. He turned instead and looked into the tunnel ahead of them. Their destination waited up there somewhere, undiscovered, unknown. He was afraid of what was ahead. He was afraid of what was behind. He was afraid to stay where they were. Yet he was intrigued. He was fascinated by what frightened him, as all people are to some small extent. All the answers lay there in that mysterious darkness, all the answers to all his questions. Surely, they must be there. He was afraid, he was unsure, he was cold, but he needed to move on. The box. The statues. This whole unearthly labyrinth. He wanted to know. But then again, who said there was a choice? There was no turning back now. There was no way out but in.

Brandy took his hand and squeezed it. Another unspoken moment passed between them, and then they began to walk, leaving the cold pool of water and the mysteries before it behind. They moved slowly, their muscles stiff from the cold, shivering and anxious, toward dangers much worse than hypothermia.

Chapter 13

Albert expected to see another statue waiting where this tunnel ended, but there was none. Instead, the tunnel made an abrupt, six-foot drop. It was almost identical to those in the first room, from which a stone finger helped him to choose. But this time there was only one choice. As he peered into the darkness below, he wondered what the purpose to such a drop might be. It seemed inconvenient, possibly even problematic, yet pointless. He remembered the two in the first room and again wondered what would have awaited them in the other tunnel.

"What's wrong?" Brandy had seen the concern upon his face, had recognized it for the same expression he'd worn several times before, including when he saw the still surface of the water and realized that their pursuer was still behind them.

"Nothing. Just wondering."

"If there's one thing I've noticed about you it's that you don't 'just wonder.'"

Albert looked at her, impressed, but trapped. "I don't know. Just something odd about this drop-off."

She peered down into it. Now she was concerned, too.

"I'll go first. You stay back a little, okay?"

"Is it safe?"

"I don't know. Probably. I'm a little on edge." He bent down, planted his hand on the floor for support and dropped into the lower passage.

"Here." Brandy knelt and held the flashlight out for him to take.

"You sure?"

She nodded.

He took the flashlight and turned back to the tunnel ahead. It was only about five feet tall, forcing him to duck down and walk with his back hunched. He took several steps forward and then stopped as his light fell on something that was lying on the floor, next to the wall.

Behind him, Brandy dropped down to follow him. "Wait up," he warned.

"What's wrong?"

Albert probed the tunnel with the flashlight, washing the walls, ceiling and floor with light, as far as it would reach, looking for something unusual, some crack or hole or crevice that might indicate some sort of trap.

Brandy looked past him to the thing on the floor. "What is it?" she asked again.

When he could find no signs of danger, he turned the light back to the small object on the floor. It was dingy white, about two inches in length. A second, smaller shard of the same material was lying next to it.

"Bone."

Brandy was silent for a moment, considering, as did he, the meaning of such a find. "Is it human?"

"I don't know."

The pieces were too big to belong to a rat, but they were only fragments. It could have been human or it could have been from a dog or a cat or a dinosaur for all he knew. In a dry tunnel like this, he didn't know how long bone fragments could last before turning to dust. And if the two of them could make it this far, any number of creatures could have done the same over the years.

Albert started forward again, sweeping the floor with his light. He felt like a soldier who has just realized that he is standing in a minefield.

"Be careful," Brandy begged him. She followed slowly, keeping some distance, but not too much. To stay behind was to be swallowed in darkness and left alone.

The tunnel was approximately forty feet in length. Along the way, Albert spied several more small bone fragments, all of them swept up against the wall like the dust that gathers around the baseboards where a vacuum cleaner doesn't quite reach. The two of them made their way to the end, stepping gingerly, holding their breath, hoping like hell that their next step did not bring death swooping out of the darkness. But death did not come. Death in this place was not so obvious.

They found themselves in a round room, standing at the mouth of one of five tunnels that led in five different directions. There were more bones here, all of them shattered fragments impossible to identify, and all of them shoved up against a surface somewhere.

Another statue stood in the center of this room, this one of five faceless sentinels. All of them were bloody and dying, with gory, ragged holes torn into their chests, backs and stomachs. One had bloody stumps for hands and one was clamoring for safety on a shredded foot. They were each reaching desperately toward one of the five tunnels.

All of these sentinels they'd encountered seemed to hold some sort of message, each one vague, but this one was obvious to Albert, and he did not need the crushed and shattered bones that littered this room to illustrate it.

"What is this place?" Brandy was gazing around at the bones and the statues, her heart pounding. She was still cold, still shivering, but she no longer noticed. There was a hot fear rising from somewhere deep inside her, and it was far more commanding than the cold.

Albert stared at the statue. "That last statue," he said, explaining as much to himself as to her. "It represented faith, sacrifice, that sort of thing. We had no choice but to go on. Something was behind us, but imagine if there hadn't been. To get this far we would've had to have faith in where we were going, in the box and all the things in it. It makes sense, really. Someone else would have turned back, tried to find another way, probably would have gotten killed somewhere along the way. We had to keep going to get this far."

Brandy nodded. She understood. "And this thing?"

Albert looked at the statue, not liking it for more than one reason. "Decisions. Deadly decisions."

"Oh good."

Albert stepped closer to the statue. The message was bad, but that was not all. He looked down at the bones at his feet, then bent and looked closer. Deep groves were carved into them, as though they'd been slashed repeatedly with a knife. As he looked closer he realized that many of them were not just broken, but *cut*. He stood up and looked at the statue again. It looked more real than the others, more *physical* somehow, and he quickly realized why. With the exception of the broken-fingered one in the first room, all the other statues were perfect, carved immaculately from stone, without a single flaw. These sentinels were scarred, and not merely by the will of the artist. Two of them were missing fingers not by design. One foot was broken off and was lying against the wall, looking morbid even in stone. They were scratched and chipped all over, as though someone had been hacking at them with a hatchet. He looked at the floor and found that it, too, was covered with faint scratches.

"So which way do we go?"

Albert lifted his eyes to the statue again. That was easy. He lifted his hand and pointed at a piece of gray cloth that hung from a sentinel's outstretched hand.

"What is that? A coat?"

Albert didn't know. It was heavy cotton, badly torn and stained. He unwound it from the statue's hand and held it before him.

"Looks kind of like part of an old Civil War jacket, doesn't it?" Brandy observed.

"Not sure," Albert replied. "Could be. Whatever it is, it's pointing the way."

Brandy leaned in to take a closer look. "How can you be sure?"

"The buttons."

And then she understood. The buttons on the fabric were simple brass with no markings, exactly like the one they'd found in the box. A closer look revealed that it was, in fact, missing one.

Albert didn't need to open the box and retrieve the button. He was certain this was their clue. He studied the garment for a moment longer, considering it. It didn't have any distinguishing designs, but only a small amount of it remained. Could it actually be a piece of a Civil War uniform? It seemed unlikely, but then again, after what he experienced in the sex room, "unlikely" had apparently taken the night off. Perhaps a unit was sent down here all those years ago to sweep the tunnels for enemy troops or supplies.

But more than likely, even if this *was* a part of a Civil War uniform, which was by no means a proven fact, it could have been worn down here by anyone in the many years after the war. Perhaps it was an old hand-me-down that kept someone warm in the winter months. Hundreds of scenarios could have brought this particular piece of fabric down here.

He reached up and hung it again on the statue's hand,

wrapping it around the wrist to keep it secure, just as he'd found it.

"You're not taking it with us?"

"No. I think we should leave it here. Maybe it'll help us find our way back out if we need it. Come on."

This next passage was easily twice as long as the one that brought them to the round room. And they had walked a little more than half the distance of the tunnel when a noise stopped them cold.

It was soft, distant, sort of like a wheel slowly rolling over dry leaves, a kind of crackling sound. It came from ahead of them and grew steadily louder, becoming more of a buzzing sound.

Brandy pressed her naked body against Albert. Neither of them spoke. This was the first noise they'd heard all night, with the exception of Albert's paint can trap, and the sudden manifestation of this unidentifiable noise was, if possible, even more frightening than the noise itself.

They watched, their eyes boring into the darkness, hunched over in the short tunnel, holding their breath and wishing their hearts would not beat so loudly, waiting for the source of the noise to appear. But as it grew closer, they realized that the noise came not from straight ahead, but from the right, on the other side of the wall. It grew until it was nearly beside them, a shuffling, clicking sort of noise that Albert could not place at all, and then it began to grow fainter, as though whatever it was had turned a corner and was now moving away from them. When it died away completely, the two of them let out the breaths they'd been holding and looked at each other.

"What was that?" Brandy did not dare to raise her voice above a whisper.

Albert shook his head. "I don't think I want to know."

"Where did it go?"

"Another tunnel somewhere. There must be miles of them."

"What if it's in the same tunnel as us? Only farther up?"

"Let's not think about that." He took her hand and led her forward, more quickly this time. He could not get the wounded statues off his mind, those deep gouges cut into solid stone. What could have made scratches like that?

A wall appeared out of the darkness ahead of them, six feet high, to the floor of another tunnel. It was identical to the place that had awaited them at the end of the flooded tunnel, but leading up instead of down.

Albert grasped the ledge and lifted himself up into the upper tunnel. It wasn't easy. He had to get a jump on it. For someone who didn't have the strength to lift their own body, this could prove a difficult, if not impossible, obstacle. He doubted if someone overweight or elderly would be able to manage it. But then again, perhaps they wouldn't have gotten this far to begin with.

Once he had his legs beneath him, he turned and took Brandy's hands, helping her up.

This tunnel was also too short to stand fully erect, so they again stood slightly hunched as they gazed into the darkness ahead. Albert looked down at the floor and noticed that there were no scratches in the stone up here. As he started forward again, he wondered why.

Chapter 14

The next room was unnervingly familiar. It was about twenty feet wide and high, far too long to see across. Like in the last room of this size, statues stood against the wall on either side, faceless sentinels posing out a dire warning.

"Oh fuck no!" blurted Brandy.

Albert stared at the statues. He could see three pairs of them, and already he knew they were different from the others. They changed, like the ones prior to the sex room, but not in the same way. These did not grow more aroused. Their penises remained limp, but their hands changed, slowly lifting from their sides, their freakish fingers curling into fists.

They moved forward, watching with mounting horror as each new pair of sentinels appeared from the gloom, acting out their warning for what lay ahead. One by one, frame by frame, each sentinel curled his hands into fists and lifted them, their long biceps swelling, straining beneath flesh of stone. The veins in their wrists and forearms popped, practically pumping with the silent pulse of a pounding stone heart. They tilted back their heads in utter rage, a silent, faceless scream, a noiseless shriek, with the cords straining on their necks and their bodies seeming to ripple with uncontrollable anger. Then they stepped away from the wall. They actually ran at their opposites, motionless frames from a horribly realistic movie, the final pair frozen in mid-stride, hell bent with murderous rage, three more steps each from killing each other.

The face that waited on the far wall did not startle them, but only because they expected it. The expression that waited there, however, scared the hell out of them. This was a different face from that in the last chamber. This was the face of a man with blazing eyes, wild hair and a lush beard. Like the face that framed the door to the sex room, it was perfect in every detail, from the hair to the eyelashes to the spittle on his lips. He looked as though he could lash out and swallow them both.

"Fuck."

Albert found Brandy's choice of words perfectly appropriate.

"Well, my dear Rudman," said Albert, doing a fairly lame Sherlock Holmes impression. "What do you surmise might happen if we enter this fellow's oral cavity?"

"I'd say we'll probably try and kill each other."

"Not good."

"No. How do we get through there?"

Albert thought for a moment, remembering the sex room and the things it made them do. They could not enter this room. If they did they'd kill each other. He couldn't imagine how, but they would, whether they meant to or not. It's what the statues told them, and so far they had not lied. "The sex room was filled with statues. It was like a big, three-dimensional porno. It got us all turned on and we couldn't control ourselves."

"That doesn't sound right."

"I know."

"I'm not going to lie, I've seen pornography before. It really doesn't have that effect on me."

He stole a glance at her, wondering. He could not imagine her sitting down to watch porn. Although the idea of her doing so was strangely arousing. Or perhaps that was just the sex room. "Maybe there was something else," he offered. "Pheromones, maybe, or something subliminal."

"Maybe all of those things to work."

"But it stopped when the lights went out," he wondered.

"Maybe it takes all those things."

"Yeah. Or maybe it's all visual." He looked at her, wondering. "Either way... When you take off your glasses, how well can you see?"

"Hardly at all. I have really bad eyes."

Albert nodded. "Nearsighted?"

"Yes."

"How far?"

"I don't know. I can see stuff, it's just all fuzzy."

"How far away are things clear? Three or four feet?"

"More like one."

"When I shined the light back in on you in the sex room, did you feel anything?"

"No. But I was scared."

"Me too, but I could have come in and done it all again as soon as I looked in there."

Brandy stared at him, shocked. She was unnerved by the fact that he felt that yearning while she was blind and scared. Could he have forced himself on her? Could he have attacked her right there and had his way with her? That would have been worse than the first time. That would have been *rape*, nothing more, nothing less.

Would someone else have done it?

"So if you take off your glasses and I close my eyes, do you think you could navigate us through this room without getting crazy?"

"I don't know. Maybe. Seems logical. I guess."

Albert looked at the man's face, considering. "That might just work." But there was something else. "The big question is, why have another one of these rooms? If we got through the other one, we're bound to know how to get through this one."

"Do you think there's something else in there?"

"Something else, something different, I don't know. I just think whoever built this place would be smarter than that."

Brandy took off her glasses and slipped them into her purse. The world around her was reduced to blurry shapes and colors. And with the exception of Albert, all of those colors were gray. "Well, I guess we have no other choice."

"Right." He took her hand and squeezed it, a sort of mental fastening of the seatbelt. "I'll keep my eyes closed. I'll be relying on you. Try not to look at anything, even if you can't see it very well."

"Okay."

Albert handed her the flashlight. "Be careful. Don't hurt yourself. Go slow and easy."

Brandy squeezed his hand in return, fastening her own mental seatbelt, and they began to walk. They stepped over the man's lips and teeth, onto his tongue and ducked into the next room. Immediately the world in front of her was a jumbled maze of gray shadows and forms. Her heart was pounding. "Still have your eyes closed?"

"Yeah, but it's tempting."

"Don't you dare!"

"Don't worry. I just mean, think about it. In our society, sex is such a big deal. Nudity is taboo. Pornography is considered filthy. We teach our kids modesty and tell them not to look at the naked women on HBO. But what if you visited a society of people who don't blush at the sight of naked bodies, who aren't ashamed of being naked or seeing someone else naked? If people just walked around naked all the time, just sat and watched people having sex all the time, had sex whenever they wanted with whomever they wanted, there would be no fascination with it. People wouldn't care. Just like seeing people kiss is no big deal to us. In a society where kissing was taboo there would be all sorts of fascination with it. So I can sort of understand that last room. I think that everybody is turned on by pornography to some small degree, even if they don't want to admit it. Even if they're more horrified and disgusted by it, they're probably still just a little turned on by it, even if that only disgusts and horrifies them more. If you were bombarded with that, life-sized, three-dimensional and in your face, and probably combined with other stuff, maybe something subconscious, something subliminal, maybe, I can almost see how that would drive us into a fit of lust and make us lose control. But this room, I don't understand. What could possibly drive us to hate? Especially if it's merely by sight?"

"I'd say it's probably best not to know." She was using the flashlight to feel her way around one of the statues. Their progress was slow, but they were getting there, and so far she felt not a shred of hate, not for Albert or otherwise.

"Yeah, you're right. The effects might be somewhat permanent."

"What do you mean?"

"Can I ask you a question?"

"Sure."

"Think about what we did back there. Just think about it a little. Are you at all turned on by that?"

Brandy blushed heavily in the darkness. She could feel the heat in her neck and face. Even so cold that she could not stop shivering, the feeling was awful. "No," she said quickly. "It was scary."

The tone of her voice told Albert he was treading on bad soil. "Oh. Okay. I could be wrong."

The two of them made their way around another large statue. They were weaving around the room, probably taking the longest possible way through it. Shadows flowed in and out of the darkness, statues in odd poses, of various heights and widths. Occasionally, a hand or a foot would materialize out of the gloom and then disappear again, and once, a face emerged, the cruel, laughing visage of a man that nearly made her scream. The very sight of that face made something stir deep in her belly, something that was not quite hatred, but something close. Resentment, perhaps, or indignity.

She pushed forward, trying to forget the disturbing face, and continued on through the strange gallery of hateful stone. It seemed to her that there were more statues in this room than there were in the sex room.

"Yes."

Albert almost opened his eyes, but was able to stop himself. "What?"

"Yes it turns me on. Really bad. But it scares me."

Albert squeezed her hand reassuringly. "Me too."

"Will we always feel like that?"

"Maybe. But if we're lucky it'll stop scaring us."

"It'll fade, too, right?"

"I'm sure it will. But whatever's in this room. That's a feeling we should never feel. Not even once. Sex can be a good thing, but hate never is."

"Do you write poems?"

"No. Why?"

"You should. You're very poetic."

"Is that a good thing?"

"It's a very good thing. It's romantic."

"Even in a hate room?"

"Yes."

Brandy felt past some stone limbs to a square opening. "I think this is the door."

"Good."

She started to go forward, but Albert pulled her back.

"Wait."

"What?"

"Don't move. Keep your back to me, don't look back, but put your glasses on and look ahead. If you see any statues, close your eyes right away and take your glasses back off."

"Why?"

"Something just feels wrong about this."

Brandy took her glasses from her purse and slid them on, then gazed through the opening and into the next room. There were no more statues. The hate room was behind them. But what she saw made her blood run cold. "Oh *god!*"

She stepped back, shoving her body against him, and he opened his eyes. Had he looked left or right he would have been face to face with the statues of the hate room, but he only looked forward. He could not take his eyes off what lay before them.

Just beyond the door, the floor dropped about ten feet into an open pit. Wicked spikes rose up from the bottom. It was a trap. Had he not stopped Brandy from going forward when he did, she would have stepped over the ledge and at the very best been speared through in a dozen places. He could not imagine her going in there and not puncturing something vital. Even if she survived the fall, it would only have been to suffer slowly until death caught up with her.

"Albert…"

"I know. It's okay."

This room of spikes was only about eight feet across, round, with a narrow ledge circling the left side, allowing access around to the next door, which was shorter than the one entering the room, no more than four feet tall.

"How did you know?"

"Like I said before, why have another room like this when, if you got past the first one, you probably knew the secret?"

"You just saved my life."

"I nearly got you killed."

She turned around and wrapped her arms around him, squeezing him so hard it hurt, and then kissed him firmly on the cheek. "Don't you dare say that!"

Albert held her, his heart pounding. Any other place, any other time, the feel of Brandy's naked body pressed against his would have made everything else in the world seem like a distant and unreachable future. He could feel her breasts against him, the subtle poke of her erect nipples, even the soft tuft of her hair against his thigh, but he noticed none of these things. He hardly even registered the kiss. All that would occupy his mind was the stone skewers rising up from the floor of that pit.

"Oh god!" cried Brandy. The words came out in a great wet sob.

"It's all right," he assured her, but he could not stop staring at the spikes.

Chapter 15

"Let's keep moving."

Brandy had been holding onto him for several minutes now, and she held him for a moment longer before moving. But she *did* begin moving, and Albert was impressed by her courage. She was scared as hell down here and had every right to be, but despite all that had happened, she just kept pushing on.

"Remember, don't look back."

She turned away and opened her eyes again. The sight of the spikes made her feel sick. The sex room was a terrible thing, an emotionally threatening trap, but this was just plain deadly. She could not help but imagine them piercing her skin, glancing off her bones, gouging her eyes, tearing her throat. The very thought made her nearly vomit with horror. How would she have gone in? Forward? Sprawled across them, the bloody tips protruding from her back in a dozen places, through her hands and thighs and head? Or would her bones have stopped her from going clear to the floor, leaving her hanging like a towel thrown over a rack to dry? Or would she have gone straight down, the spikes ramming through the arches of her bare feet, entering the meat of her calf or thighs and sliding mercilessly up the bones? Would it have killed her instantly, spearing her brain or her heart? Or would she have hung there, twitching and gagging while blood gushed from her mouth, the pain unbearable but unending? The scenarios would not end.

Had she taken just one more step…

Albert measured up the path around the spikes. The ledge was narrow, but it wouldn't be a problem. It was designed to trip up someone stepping out of there in the dark. For someone who knew what they were doing, it was simply a matter of walking around it.

Brandy stepped out of the hate room, her thoughts still lingering on the death she'd narrowly avoided. With her back to the wall, taking no more chances than necessary with the deadly pit, she began to move around the narrow ledge, circling the left side of the room to the doorway on the other side, which was actually a short tunnel, about three feet long.

The next room was about twice as large as the pit room with an identical doorway on the other side and a tall ceiling. It was completely empty. Brandy looked at Albert and noticed the expression on his face, that same concerned look that said something was not right. Looking at the room, she understood why. Before now the only places without something in it, be it statues or a pit of spikes or a pool of water, were the corridors that led from one room to the next. So why leave *this* room empty?

"Another trap?"

Albert shook his head. "I don't know." He looked around the room, searching for something different, some stone out of place or unusual holes or slots, but that did not seem right either. The traps Indiana Jones faced in the Temple of Doom were extravagant, consisting of stone mechanics dating thousands of years in the past. He honestly did not expect to have arrows fly out at him or the walls to begin moving, but what else could a seemingly empty room contain? He steeled himself and stepped forward.

"Albert, no!"

"It's okay. Just wait there." He was scared. He was damn scared. With every step he expected to be impaled or crushed or worse. It was the same fear he'd felt before removing the bags from the praying statue's hands. Back then he'd felt silly afterwards, wondering how he could expect such deadly consequences, but that was before he discovered what lay beyond the hate room. This place was getting more dangerous by the minute. But Brandy was the one who almost paid the price for pushing forward, and he would be damned if he was going to let her take any more chances.

No spikes impaled him. The ceiling did not come down on top of him. No fireball set him ablaze. The room was just a room and nothing more. Beyond it, the next passage was identical to the one that led back to the pit.

He paused in the middle of the room, gazing down the next corridor, wishing he'd taken the light from

Brandy so that he could see how far the next tunnel went. It was now that he felt something, a paranoid sense that they were not alone in this small room. He lifted his gaze upward, into the darkness above him.

Brandy saw him look up and quickly shined the light up to the high ceiling.

There was nothing there. Not a thing.

Yet Albert would have sworn…

Nothing.

He turned and walked quickly back to where Brandy stood. Still waiting for the end to fall upon him from some unseen crevice, he took her hand and the two of them crossed the room and entered the next tunnel.

Albert looked back as they left the chamber behind. It wasn't right. There was something terribly wrong about that room. He could feel it. Yet they passed through it without harm.

Perhaps he was only being paranoid.

As they approached the end of the corridor, they heard the same shuffling, clicking, crackling noise that frightened them in the earlier passage. The sound more distant than before, but grew louder as they walked.

It was enough to tear their thoughts from both the deadly spikes and the mysteriously empty room.

"Albert…"

"I know." Albert squinted into the darkness ahead. Whatever that noise was, they were walking straight toward it.

When they reached the end of the tunnel and stepped out into the next chamber, neither of them were able to quite believe what greeted them. Stretched out before them was what appeared to be an enormous stone bridge, nearly thirty feet wide, vanishing into the darkness ahead. On each side ran a low wall, beyond which was nothing but darkness. And it was impossible to tell just how high up the ceiling was. The flashlight simply didn't reach.

Without speaking, they turned and walked over to the edge of the bridge and peered over with the flashlight. Stretched out below them, as far as the light would reach, was an enormous stone maze.

"Wow," exclaimed Albert. He could only see the tops of the walls, but that was enough to reveal that the passages were narrow. It was impossible to see a path through it from up here, much less from within those high walls.

It was from this maze that the strange noises came.

"I never would have imagined that something this big could be down here." He looked up at the darkness above them. "How far underground are we?"

Brandy was staring down at the maze. She did not really care how far down they were. What she was concerned with was that noise. "What's down there?" Her voice was barely a whisper.

"I don't know, but I hope it can't climb. Come on."

The two of them began to cross the bridge, but something far to their right caught Albert's eye and he stopped.

"What is it?" Brandy stopped and followed his gaze. When she shined the flashlight at it, her stomach began to churn again. "Albert, those are our clothes!"

It wasn't all their clothes, but it *was* their undergarments. An enormous pillar, at least as big around as a city water tower, stood just within the reach of the flashlight. Three white socks were hung on the side facing them. Above these, hanging side-by-side, were Albert's white briefs and Brandy's flowered white panties. Higher up hung Brandy's bra. The last sock must have fallen into the shadows with the things that were making the noise.

"How do we get to them?" Brandy caught herself trying to cover her nakedness again. Apparently, just the sight of some of her clothing was enough to remind her that she was stark naked and her male companion could see her most private parts.

Albert shook his head. "I don't think we do."

There were things moving down there, unseen in the shadows. Albert could hear them prowling the narrow passageways in the dark. It was impossible to say how many there were.

"Why would somebody put them there?"

"Maybe to give those things our scent."

Brandy glanced at him and then looked back at their unreachable undergarments. "I don't like the sound of that."

"Neither do I." He also didn't like how the clothes were hung as they would be wearing them if they were down there. It looked to him as though someone had tried to simulate their presence.

Scent doubles, he thought, and shivered.

He took Brandy's hand and led her across the bridge, trying not to look at the maze below. But he could not forget those undergarments. Why only those items? Why not use all their clothes?

Three passages awaited them, framed by four sentinels. All four were identical, feet together, hands at their sides. They were neither in motion nor amorous, but they were also not helping them.

"So which one do we take?" Brandy asked.

"I'm not sure." He removed his backpack, knowing well where the answer would be if there was one.

The finger and the button had been used, and he doubted if they would come into play again, but he kept them just in case. This left only the knife blade, the watch and the feather. He removed these three items and examined each of them. But nothing about them gave him any clues.

He walked to the nearest passage and peered inside, looking for anything out of place. Brandy followed him, lending him light. "You figured all the others out. You can get this one."

"I hope so." He moved on to the second passage and then the third. Nothing.

Brandy turned her light to the statues, searching them for any slight difference. So far, they seemed to each have all their parts. None of them were missing a finger.

Albert shook his head. "So far they've been pretty easy clues. Whoever gave us that box wanted us to get this far, and I don't see why we should stop here." He gazed out at the darkness that loomed over the maze beyond the side of the bridge. Somewhere, one of the things began making its strange shuffling and clicking sound. There was also a sound like stone striking stone, over and over again, very rapidly.

He turned away from the maze and began examining the statue on the far left.

"Hey." Brandy was standing on her toes beside the statue on the far right, shining her light up at the statue's neck. "Look at this."

Albert hurried to her side and stretched up on his own toes to see what she was looking at.

"See it? Something's scratched into its neck."

"Yeah, I do." He grasped the statue's arm and craned

his neck to see. It looked as if someone had taken a sharp tool and etched something into the stone there, almost like a tattoo. "It looks like…"

Brandy lifted the light up as high as she could and focused it on the mark.

"It looks like a bird," he decided at last. It was a crude image, but once he wrapped his head around it there was no denying. He could make out what was supposed to be wings and a beak.

"Bird," Brandy repeated. "Bird feather!"

Albert nodded. "I think so. Good eyes. You rock."

"Naturally." She gave him a cool wink and he again felt a spark of arousal. Was that the sex room lingering in him? Or was it just him? At that moment, he could not say. She was proud of herself for finding one of the clues and for that moment she seemed more confident, more in control. And it looked damn good on her. And it wasn't as if he hadn't been crushing on her even before they entered the sex room. Maybe it was just his natural attraction to her. Or maybe the sex room simply amplified that.

"Must be the tunnel on the right then," he surmised,

suppressing his feelings. Walking around naked didn't leave any room to be turned on, not when you were a man in flesh and blood. He almost envied the statues for that advantage.

"I guess so," Brandy agreed.

Below them there was a violent outburst, a rapid clattering arose, as if a great many things were clashing together over and over again at high speeds. It sounded eerily like hundreds of blades beating together, as though there were an intense battle raging far below them without a sound but for the swords clanging upon one another.

"We should go," Albert urged.

Brandy glanced one last time toward the sprawling maze and then followed him into the tunnel, leaving the noises for the darkness.

Chapter 16

The passage was about eight feet tall by five feet in width when they entered, but as they walked, the ceiling sloped gradually downward and the walls slowly closed, narrowing until they could no longer walk fully upright or side-by-side.

Before the tunnel grew too small, Albert stopped and peered back the way they'd come, a little unnerved by the claustrophobic position they were finding themselves in.

"Are we going the right way?" Brandy asked, noticing his hesitance.

Albert shook his head. "We have to be," he replied. "There was a bird."

Brandy giggled a little at how absurd that sounded.

"It was the only clue we had."

"I know."

"We have to be going the right way. Do you want to lead or follow?"

Brandy looked back the way they'd come, and then up ahead at where they were going. On one hand there was the fear of what may lie ahead, the anxious unknowing, the danger, but on the other hand there was the question of what may be behind them, the thought that she may be vulnerable. "How narrow do you think it'll get?"

"Hard to say. We may have to crawl soon."

She took a deep breath and decided: "I'll go first." It was the thought of being blind on two sides, unable to either turn around or see past Albert that ultimately decided it for her. She squeezed past him and pushed forward.

Albert removed the backpack and followed.

As the walls closed in around her, forcing her to duck lower and lower, Brandy's anxiety grew. She was not usually claustrophobic, but she was feeling that suffocating feeling now. What if it grew too narrow to fit through? What if they became stuck down here, perhaps miles underground, in a place no one else on earth even knew existed? She did not like the thought of the irony of narrowly surviving that pit of spikes only to slowly die of thirst wedged between these walls. She shook away the thought, and asked Albert where he thought the other two tunnels led.

"I don't know. If I had to guess I'd say probably down to that maze. That seemed like a good place for getting rid of trespassers."

"Do you think every choice we didn't make was a trap?"

"I don't know. Maybe not. Whoever took our clothes could have gone a different way. Maybe we got the hard road and he's taking the easy one."

"I don't like not knowing who's in here with us."

"I don't either."

The ceiling had finally descended too low for them to walk and they dropped to their hands and knees. Albert had to place his backpack on the floor beneath him and drag it along between his hands. This was awkward, but he managed to keep up.

Ahead of them, the tunnel made a sharp right turn and then continued down the ever-shrinking corridor. It was about now, as they made this tight turn, that Albert became distracted by the view. He was staying close behind Brandy, not wanting to be left behind, and he found himself staring at her round buttocks and the titillating slit of her vagina that her crawling posture revealed. Even without a flashlight he could see that part of her perfectly in the backlight. The muscles of her thighs pumped solidly as she crawled, stretching and contracting in a motion that was incredibly erotic. The sight sent a knot into his stomach and he forced his eyes back down to the floor. He felt guilty looking at her that way. It was ungentlemanly as all hell, but it was also a damn pleasant distraction from his fear of this labyrinth.

The walls and ceiling closed in around them until they had to give up crawling on hands and knees to continue on their bellies, and Albert's view of Brandy was thankfully replaced by a much less interesting view of his backpack as he shoved it forward ahead of him.

"I see the end of the tunnel," Brandy reported. They were sweet words to Albert. "Only a little farther."

"Thank God," Albert sighed. "I'm starting to get claustrophobic."

"Me too."

The last few feet were a squeeze, but they managed to make it through without getting stuck. The only truly difficult part was exiting the tunnel itself. The floor of the next room was several feet lower than the floor of the tunnel. Brandy slithered from a hole much smaller than the one they entered, inching her way out until she could plant her hands on the cold floor and ease herself down. It was now that she wished that she had opted to go second so that Albert could have given her a hand, but she couldn't change that now.

Albert pushed his backpack through the hole after her and immediately began to pull himself free. Claustrophobia had begun to get the best of him and he wanted out as quickly as possible.

Brandy grabbed the backpack as she stood and tried to give him a hand, but he was on the floor before she could get a grip on him. She heard something strike the floor way too hard—his elbow, she thought—but he did not seem to notice. He was already studying this newest chamber.

This room was round, its diameter at least sixty feet. A walkway about ten feet wide circled the room, as did dozens of tunnel entrances identical to the one they just exited. In the center of the room, a steep, spiraling staircase sank down into the darkness below and at the top of these steps stood a lone sentinel statue. It was standing upright and stiff, with its feet together, facing the top of the staircase. Its right hand was at its side, but the left was raised toward the steps, its grotesquely long index finger extended.

"I think it wants us to go down," said Brandy. Her eyes fell to the statue's penis again. There was a grotesque sort of eroticism about a penis that big. It stirred something in her gut, something as unpleasant and unavoidable as a nicotine craving, and she wondered if it was the sex room again. "Do you think we should?"

"I don't know," replied Albert as he clambered to his feet. "So far they seem to be on our side, but we'll have a look in all the passages anyway. Just in case."

"We should mark the tunnel we came in through."

"With what? I left the spray paint behind."

Brandy handed Albert the flashlight, and then removed a tube of lipstick from her purse. She scrawled a glossy X on the wall on each side of the tunnel and then replaced the tube.

"I'm impressed."

"I know."

Albert laughed.

It took him only a moment to check out all of the passages that led away from the stairs. Nothing but smooth, clean stone could be seen in each of them. But he hadn't really expected to see anything. The statue was pointing down and he had a strong hunch that if they were going to get through this labyrinth alive, they would do well to trust these faceless beings.

He turned and peered down into the darkness below, trying to judge how far down it could go, but it was impossible.

"So why is it that this guy points the way but all the others were all mysterious about it?"

Albert shrugged. "Maybe he figures by now we've earned it." He handed the flashlight back to her and began to lead the way down the spiraling steps, descending ever farther into the unknown.

Chapter 17

"God, I need a cigarette," gasped Brandy. She paused and gazed up at the dizzying spiral of steps above them. It felt like they'd descended at least twenty stories. The steps were both steep and narrow, demanding careful treading to prevent a deadly fall into the abyss below, and her legs and back ached from the effort.

Albert went a few steps farther and then stopped and sat down. He looked up above him at the distance they'd covered, huffing exhaustedly. He wished there was some way of knowing just how deep they were. It felt like they just kept going down.

"It's unbelievable," gasped Brandy. "How much deeper can we possibly go?"

Albert shook his head. He had no idea.

She sat down on the steps to catch her breath. "We can't just go down forever, can we?"

"You wouldn't think." Albert gazed down into the darkness. There was no telling what might lie at the bottom of this hole, but he was certain of one thing: there were still two clues left in the box. He was sure they would have to use both of them before they reached the end of this labyrinth.

He turned and looked at Brandy, who was leaning back on the steps with her arms at her sides and her knees together, staring up into the darkness from which they'd come. She was slick with perspiration and her breasts were rising and falling with her labored breath. He watched her for a moment, taking in her beauty, and then turned his gaze back to the emptiness below.

"Thank you," he said after a moment.

Brandy sat up and looked down at him. "Why?"

"For not leaving me back there after the sex room. I would've let you."

Brandy looked down at the flashlight. She remembered him telling her that she could take it and go, that she could just leave him down here in the darkness. She'd actually been tempted to do just that. Now she felt ashamed of that urge. "I couldn't have done that," she said at last, and realized that it was the truth. "I couldn't have gotten out on my own. I would've been too scared." She looked at him again, but he was not looking back at her. "Besides, I couldn't just leave you there. What if you never came back? You couldn't have found your way out of here in the dark and I never could've lived with myself for just leaving you to die."

Albert stared into the darkness. "But I could've been the bad guy."

"I don't think you are. If you were, I think I would've found out before now."

"You could've called the police. They would've come to get me."

"True. But what if they came down here and found you dead?"

Albert could think of no response for that.

"Then I'd live with the guilt for sure and they'd probably put me away for abandoning you like that."

"I'm sure they would've understood."

"Can we please not talk about this? It's upsetting me."

"I'm sorry."

"Don't be." She smiled a little. Perhaps he *was* the bad guy, but if so, he was hiding it very well. It didn't really matter anyway. By the time they'd reached the sex room, she was already at his mercy and would be until they were back above ground.

And so far he'd been a perfect gentleman. Except for that whole sex room thing, of course. But she hadn't exactly played hard-to-get back there.

No, he didn't fit the part of a killer. In fact, he was the only thing making her feel remotely safe down here. Although she *would* admit that his ability to solve the puzzles in this place was extremely creepy at times.

"Ready to go on?" Albert asked, standing up.

"Yeah."

The two of them had barely completed another lap around the hole when the ground finally came into view.

A short passage led into the next room and as Albert peered inside, he saw that it was cavernous, perhaps the size of the maze they spied from the bridge, its ceiling far too high to see with what light they carried.

"Wow."

"Yeah." Albert gazed around at the room as he passed through it. He expected to find something down here. He expected to see a statue materialize out of the gloom, another bridge, more water, some sort of obstacle to overcome, but the room was empty. Again Albert felt that strange sense of wrongness. This room shouldn't have been here. It served no visible purpose, yet here it was. He looked around, paranoid, feeling as though something was watching them, waiting for them to drop their guard, perhaps.

But there was nothing.

Before them appeared a huge wall of stone and a small corridor leading through it. There was nothing more to the room. It was just a vast, empty space. Albert supposed that it could have been intended for some purpose other than traps and obstacles. It could have been a banquet hall of some sort, for example. But he didn't think so. Nothing else in this labyrinth seemed to serve any purpose other than to impede their way forward.

They ducked into the short passage in the far wall

and into the next room. Here, they stopped and stood. Albert's musings about the empty room behind them vanished from his thoughts at once. They stood side-by-side, staring forward, neither of them surprised, but both of them nearly sick at the reality of the sight before them.

"Fuck."

"Fuck," Albert agreed.

The room was twenty feet high and twenty feet wide. Too far to see the other end. Three pairs of sentinels were visible, lined up against the walls on either side. The first were standing straight, their feet together, hands at their sides, grotesquely long penises limp and pointed at the floor. Like their brothers in the last two rooms like this, each pair was slightly different than the one before.

What more could this hellish place give them? It already drove them to lust and tried to make them hate. But Albert already knew what was coming. He knew because he was surprised it wasn't the first.

Brandy took his hand and the two of them started forward, watching as the sentinels slowly mimed out their message. They raised their hands, not to threaten, as they did the last time, but to defend. They bent their knees and sank into a crouch as their long, thin arms crossed before their empty faces. Soon they were sitting, their knees sprawled out, their faces uplifted in an expressionless shriek. There was no aggression in them now. The final pair of sentinels sat with their backs arched and their necks stretched out as they threw their heads back in what could only have been a howl of such ferocious terror that even without faces, they appeared to have completely plunged into madness.

The face that appeared in the far wall made their stomachs boil with acid, their hearts pound like machines and their skin tingle with gooseflesh despite the sweat clinging to their weary bodies. It was the face of a woman, but different from the first one. This woman was heavier, her face rounder, her features pudgier. She was fairer than the lusting woman and had a mole under her right eye. Her mouth was open in a frozen and silent scream so fierce that, had she been real, her vocal cords could not possibly have gone undamaged. Her eyes bulged with terror, her lips peeled back. It was the face of sudden madness, of fright so terrible it could kill.

"Albert, I don't know if I can."

"Of course you can."

"No. I'm scared."

"So am I."

"Please, Albert."

He turned and squeezed her hand. "This has got to be the last one. The only emotion as powerful as lust, hate and fear is love and I doubt if Cupid's got a pad down here." It was a lie though. He was sure that any mind sick enough to create these three rooms was also capable of forcing other emotions into dangerous levels. Sorrow, and even joy, could become too much to bear under the right circumstances.

She stared at him, pleading with her eyes, and it broke his heart.

"You did wonderful in the hate room. You didn't feel any hate at all."

"But I didn't feel any hate *before* I went in. I'm *already* scared."

"But you won't be any more scared if you don't let yourself be. I'll be right beside you, holding onto you the whole time. I promise."

She stared at him, suddenly trembling with fright. "I

don't know."

"I do. You're a brave girl. I've seen it."

"I'm scared."

"I know."

"What if I can't go on? What if we get in there and I can't go any farther?"

"Then we'll turn around."

She stared up at him, her eyes pleading. "Promise?"

"Promise. I wouldn't make you go on. You know that." He gazed into her eyes, pleading with her. "I just want you to try."

Brandy *did* know that. Even in the short time they'd spent together in this strange labyrinth of stone, she somehow *knew* that he would take care of her. Something deep inside her heart knew with certainty that he was not deceiving her.

She took a deep breath, gathered strength from his touch and his honest eyes and then removed her glasses. She stepped up to the woman's face and stared at her, terrified of what lay waiting in her throat.

Albert stepped behind her and put his hands on her bare hips. "I'm right behind you."

"You said earlier, before we went into the hate room…why have another room like this when, if you got through one, you probably knew the secret?"

"Yes I did."

"Well?"

"I'm right here. I'm not going to let anything hurt you. Be as careful as you can. Watch where you step; watch what you touch. I'll be right here the whole time."

She took another deep breath and stepped into the woman's mouth.

Chapter 18

Shapes in gray materialized as Brandy entered the fear room. For the first time in her life, she wished her eyes were actually *worse* than they were. A single stone statue stood before her. She could not tell if it was male or female, human or otherwise, but its arms were outstretched, almost a cruciform pose. She felt her way around it, gently feeling her way across the floor, her bare toes tracing the unseen path before her.

This room was bigger than the others. She could feel it. All around her, limbs were reaching toward her. She turned right, then left, then right again, slipping around statues of things she knew would drive her mad if she could see them.

Seeking distraction, she began to sing softly to herself as she walked, trying to focus on the words to Robert Frost's poem, "The Road Less Traveled," that she used to sing in choir when she was in high school.

An aisle spread out before her between the gray forms, and the silhouette of a woman appeared at its end. This woman was on her knees, bent painfully backward. Brandy could barely see it, but from her angle the profile of the breasts and chin and upturned face were clear, and she could only imagine what might have caused her to take that pose. Something was standing in front of the woman, something big and animal-like, something that she could not make out at all, but that scared her nonetheless, as though the shape reminded her of something, something locked away deep in her mind, something forgotten all her life, too terrible to remember.

"How are you doing?" Albert asked.

"Okay. I'm scared. I don't think this room's as nice as the last one. It still scares me."

"That's because you're scared of it."

"No. There's something else."

There was a pause from Albert as he considered this

and then, "Just hang in there, okay?"

"Okay."

"And be careful."

"I am."

Every step was painfully cautious, her mind flooded with agonizing certainty that the next would bring unspeakable pain. Beneath her bare feet was cool stone, smooth and hard, and she tried to focus on that, tried to see only the floor, the flat, cold surface that could be her undoing if it should suddenly end, but all around her, hulking figures loomed, figures that were almost unseen by her poor eyes, but were there nonetheless, as much in her mind as in the room. She felt Albert squeeze her hips reassuringly and tried to focus on that, tried to focus on *him*, on his companionship, on his friendship, on his courage, and when she could not, she focused on his sexuality, on the sex room and what they'd done together. She forced herself to remember how he felt inside her, how they'd attacked each other and did what could not possibly be called making love even by the most perverse joker. They "fucked." That's what they did. The two of them, no telling how many miles underground, in a room full of stone pornography, threw away all their modesty and shame and morals and they fucked each other like animals. She recalled the act—what she could remember of it—and focused on it, though she'd hardly let herself think of it until now. She grew hot, her stomach knotting. She reminded herself that they were still naked and that she could have him again if she wanted. He wouldn't turn her down, not even down here. She reminded herself of this and it made her hotter, more excited. She could have turned around and fucked him again, as hard and loveless as she did in the sex room, right there amid the ageless terror of the fear room. She knew she could. That sexuality scared her. That excitement terrified her. The effects of the sex room were still with her and embracing it was like embracing a deadly sea snake, its slimy, coiling body writhing against her skin, but she embraced it nonetheless. She *gorged* herself on it, for the fear of her lust was not as great as her fear of the fear. Yet the terror of the fear room was still there. The fear still surrounded her. Even unrestrained lust could not push it back entirely.

She stopped. Before her, amid the dark, shapeless

forms, something stood blocking her path, something that was a good head shorter than she, but made up for its height in breadth. She told herself she could see nothing, not a thing, only shadows and forms and blurry gray blobs, but she could not take her eyes off it. It was familiar to her, like a forgotten childhood boogeyman lurking in the closet, peering out at her from the darkness and grinning hungrily. A memory rushed back to her, a memory buried so deep inside her brain that it could not possibly have been her own. A cloudless sky, a burning sun, dunes of sand... She closed her eyes and forced away the image. That memory was not her own. That was the memory of a desert and she had never in her life been to a desert. But the image persisted. There was something in the sand, something hungry and clever and merciless.

"What's wrong?"

She realized that she was standing motionless, completely distracted by those creepy thoughts. "Nothing," she replied. But it wasn't nothing. She started forward again, walking around the stone creature. She did not look at it again. She kept her eyes aimed firmly forward, yet it was still there, tempting her. She could see things in her mind, horrible things, things (screaming, terrible screaming) that could only be from her own imagination but somehow weren't. These things were all real. She slipped around the statue, turned to avoid another one and was suddenly in a corner of stone. Blurred faces stared back at her, all of them screaming, some in terror, some in terrible glee, others in complete madness. Panic shot through her like an electric bolt.

"*Albert*!"

"I'm here." He could feel her rapid breathing. He pulled her back against him and felt the hammering of her heart.

"The path is blocked!"

"It's okay. Just backtrack a little."

"I can't!"

He let go of her hips and slipped his arms around her, hugging her. "They're just stone. This room's just an obstacle. We can get past it."

Brandy shook her head. "I'm too scared."

"It's okay."

"I can't."

He hugged her closer. "You're braver than this. I

know you are. You're the bravest girl I've ever known. Look what you've already done. Don't let some stupid statues get the better of you." These were big words to speak for someone as scared as he was. He told her to go on, begged her to get a grip and keep moving, but his own brain was screaming at him to turn back. He could not see the statues at all, and still he was afraid. He could not imagine how terrified she must be, seeing all the things she saw, even with her eyes in her purse and the world a permanent cloud of haze. "I know you're stronger than that," he whispered into her ear.

Brandy sniffed back the tears that had formed in her eyes. The terror was intense, but Albert was right. They were just stone, and reason was reason. They could not hurt her. "Okay."

Albert dropped his arms from around her and grasped her hips again, and then the two of them turned and backtracked.

The statues in the sex room were a jumbled mess, but it was a mess that was reasonably easy to navigate. The hate room was worse, but she had assumed it was because she was blind. Now she realized that the rooms were getting more complicated, each one designed to be more of a maze than the last. She wondered what would happen if they could not find their way back and quickly forced that thought away.

An odd form appeared ahead of her and to her right. It seemed human, but oddly stretched out of proportion. She stared at it for a moment before it occurred to her that this was one of the sentinels. He stood amid shorter statues, straight and tall, his arms outstretched over the heads of those formless things around him.

She went toward him, wondering. There were none of these statues in the sex room. Those were all human.

But she did not dwell on the statue's presence for long. Behind it, she saw another statue that was clearly not human. It was close to the floor, spread out across the space it occupied, and there, just beyond *this* creature, was a square opening, barely visible to her poor eyes in the pale light.

"I found the door!"

"Look first."

Brandy was already taking her glasses from her purse. "We're not there yet." She stepped around the sentinel, forcing herself to move slowly, watching each step, knowing that to forget the hate room was to forget to survive.

She edged around the last statue, a beast that reminded her of an animal, but seemed twice as wide as it should have been. She brushed it with her leg and felt a sharp pain.

"Ouch!"

"What's wrong?"

She touched her leg where the pain was and lifted her finger in front of her face. She was bleeding, but not badly. "I cut myself."

"*What*?"

"It's not bad," she assured him. "It was a statue. It's got a claw or something. Be careful."

"Okay."

She pushed forward, encouraged by the sight of the door just ahead of her.

"We're here," she announced.

"Be careful."

She slipped the glasses onto her face and peered into the next room as she did in the hate room. She knew her mistake at once, but there was no undoing it. She turned, her eyes squeezed fiercely shut against the image that was already burned into her brain, and threw herself into Albert's arms.

Albert stumbled backward a step, startled, and his eyes flew open.

He saw what Brandy had seen. He saw it clearly, even though the flashlight was sandwiched between their bodies, its beam reduced to a narrow slit.

This door did not exit the fear room. It entered another chamber of it.

The next room was narrow and curved, filled with more statues like those that surrounded them. One stood out from the others, the first in the room, looming in front of them. He closed his eyes at once, frightened so badly he could not bear to look upon it, but still he saw the horrible image. In his head it went on and on, his mind unable to close its eye.

The statue showed a woman, naked like all the rest down here. Her face was contorted into an expression of terror and agony. She was up to her waist in a hole in the floor. Curved spikes rose from the rim of this hole and dug cruel gouges into the flesh of her hips and waist. Three other people, two men and one woman, each as naked as the day they were born, were shoving her down into the hole from where grotesque things that looked like something between tentacles and talons clawed at her, pulling her to her death below. The statue could have been the work of any artist obsessed with the macabre except for the terrifying detail. The terror and pain on the woman's face and the mad glee in the eyes of her murderers were too intense, too *real* for anyone other than a madman to recreate. But there was more to the statue than just the intensity and the reality. There was something much deeper than just the image. What startled him, what terrified him beyond his imagination, was the *familiarity* of the statue. This scene was not something merely imagined by some mad artist. This was a life-sized portrait of the past. Somewhere, sometime, lost in eternity, this event really took place. The murderers were real. The woman was real. The thing in the hole was real...

A sound escaped him, a shrill utterance that might have been a scream or might have been a laugh or might have been his sanity fleeing his skull. He held Brandy tightly in his arms and tried to force away the thing he saw, but he couldn't.

"*I want to go home!*" Brandy sobbed. She was crying, terrified not only by what she saw but by what she remembered, by what she could not possibly have known but somehow did.

"Okay." The mystery of this place seemed unimportant now. Nothing mattered now except getting home. He did not care where the box came from or why it and the key were given to them. He did not want to go any farther. "Okay let's go."

She did not move. She held fast to him, her naked body pressed firmly against his.

"You have to lead us back out."

"*I can't!*"

"You have to."

"*I can't! I can't go! I'm too scared!*"

"I can't get us out of here, Brandy!"

"*I can't!*" Her tears coursed down his chest. She was terrified beyond the limits of her courage. She could not turn back and face those things she'd stumbled past again.

He wanted to run, to just turn and flee back the way they'd come. Had he been capable, he might have left her there in the darkness, crying and screaming until she died of fright, but he could not do that. He could not leave her there. He picked her up instead, cradling her in his arms, and began to walk back the way they'd come.

He banged his leg against the statue that cut Brandy a few moments ago and felt the same sharp pain. Whatever it was, it was covered with claws or spikes or something. He could feel the blood trickling down his leg and the pain magnified the fear.

But he couldn't run. To run would be to lose control. To lose control would be to die. This was no exaggeration and he knew it. Fear alone could kill and this place was terror in its purest form.

A blind man in a tomb of monsters, he walked. His eyes tightly shut against the terrors that surrounded them. Brandy still held the flashlight, and to look would be to invite madness. He stumbled through the dark, guiding himself only with his feet, feeling his way around statue after statue, trying to walk only in one direction, only in the direction from which they'd come, and found only one obstacle after another. His feet struck stone limbs and more than once he bumped Brandy's shoulder or leg into one of the many solid occupants of the room.

Panic welled up within him. He did not know the way out. He had a sick feeling he was only going in circles, that the two of them would be trapped in this room for hours, unable to find their way either forward or backward.

He wondered if his heart could actually last that long.

"Are we out yet?"

"I can't find the way out."

"What do we do?" She spoke in great, wet sobs.

"Just keep your eyes shut. Nothing can hurt you here. I'll get us out."

"Hurry. Please."

Albert knew there was only one way out, and he knew that way might ruin him, turning his brain to mush, rendering him little more than a drooling shell. The terrors in here were never meant to be looked upon. But there was Brandy to think about. Even if it killed him, he had to look. He had to find the door.

He steeled himself and took several deep, calming breaths. He tried to find reason in the madness, some ray of hope, and found one in remembering the sex room. Those statues did not take effect at first. They had time to study the statues, to examine them for what they were before their libidos went into overdrive. He took one more deep breath and, against his every instinct, he opened his eyes.

The door was in front of him, slightly to his right. It was only five or six steps away. But between it and him stood a great, twisted shape that sent a jolt of utter horror straight through his very soul.

It was facing the other way, toward the door, poised to greet anyone coming in. Albert was staring at the twisted, boiling flesh of its back, unable to see its face, and still it terrified him. He might has well have opened his eyes and gazed upon the real thing as it stumbled toward him, inches from rending the flesh from his face.

He squeezed his eyes shut again, but it was too late. His mind was filled with horrors that he could not unsee. It was as if he actually lived through the terrors this statue depicted. The visions in his head (Dead! They're all dead!) were as vivid as his own memories. He shuddered with fright, fighting to keep his grip on Brandy, trying to keep his own legs from collapsing beneath him. How was this happening? How did these horrible images (So many of them!) get into his head? It couldn't be real. It had to be (They won't die!) some kind of hallucination.

Somehow, he managed to take a step forward, and then another. His feet felt numb. He could not feel the floor beneath him anymore. His knees were shaking. He opened his eyes again and tried to stare only at the doorway. That was his only goal. He just needed to reach the doorway. If he could just get Brandy that far, then even if he dropped dead of fright, at least she'd have a chance at getting home.

His stomach boiled with fear. His head pounded. He walked forward, unable to completely ignore the things around him. Even from the corners of his eyes he saw them, those terrible images of death and blood and creatures from a past he was never meant to know.

He already knew that these things would haunt his dreams for the rest of his life.

Albert emerged from the door of the fear room, stepping over the stone tongue and teeth of the woman whose horrible fate he'd almost shared. Brandy's frail, trembling body still cradled in his arms, he walked shivering away from the mysteries that lay beyond.

They had forfeited.

Game over.

Chapter 19

Albert did not stop when he stepped out of the fear room. He walked on, Brandy's trembling body still held tightly against him, the flashlight still pressed between them. "It's okay," he told her. "We're out. We're okay." He kept telling her this, kept assuring her, but he felt like a liar. It *was* okay. They *were* out. But he did not yet know if *he* would ever be okay again. Images haunted his mind. His head ached. His back ached the way it did when one shivered too hard for too long. His very lungs seemed to ache with fright.

There were things in his thoughts now, shadowy things, like dark memories struggling to surface. He tried to stare forward, tried to look only where he was going, trying to suppress the urge to shriek in utter terror.

The fear did not begin to subside until after he passed the last of the sentinels and entered the passage that led to the next room. It was then that he finally looked down at Brandy and found that she was staring up at him, her blue eyes shadowy in the darkness, but still as soft and brilliant as ever. The expression on her face was impossible to read. It could have been relief, it could have been gratitude, it could have been love or it could have been nothing at all. She made no effort to be put down, and he made no effort to put her down. He walked on through the huge and unsettlingly empty room to the spiraling staircase from which they'd descended, cradling her in his arms, liking the way she felt, letting her body's weight and softness and warmth occupy his mind so that the terrors could not grow. He climbed seven of the steep steps before finally stopping and lowering her gently onto them, as though unwilling to set her on the same floor as those terrible statues.

For a moment he stood staring at her. She lay before him, staring back at him, her hands clamped around the flashlight at her bosom, one leg dangling off the edge of the staircase, the other bent slightly, her foot resting on the step below her. Her hair was still kinky from their earlier swim and her skin was pocked with gooseflesh. He could see the slit of her sex between her parted thighs, uncovered, unhidden, but he felt not a trace of the sex room's arousal at the sight. He saw only her beauty, her anguish, her need. He needed to take care of her. She depended on him, just as he depended on her. Without each other they neither one would make it back to the surface. They were right to turn around. The answers weren't worth it. They didn't matter. All that mattered was Brandy. All that mattered was Albert. The two of them were the only things down here that mattered at all and he intended to get them both safely home.

He bent and took her hands, wrapping them in his so that she did not have to release the flashlight she was still clutching. Her cheeks were still wet with the tears she'd cried in the fear room, but she was not crying now.

"I'm sorry," she said.

He shook his head. "Don't be." He smiled the best smile he could manage to reassure her, and it touched his heart when she gave him a little smile back. "Let's get you home."

As she let him help her to her feet, she happened to glimpse the blood on his knee. "You're hurt…"

Albert looked down at his leg. He'd hardly realized. "I bumped into that statue that cut you."

Brandy looked down at her own leg. Just above her right knee, on the outer thigh, there were three small cuts. The top one had bled a small trail down over the lower two, but those had just barely beaded with blood. The cuts on Albert's left knee, however, were considerably deeper. A trail of blood ran all the way down to his ankle.

"I'm okay," he assured her. "It's not bleeding anymore."

But she wasn't entirely convinced. Her cuts had stung. They *still* stung, now that she thought about it. No matter what he said, his *had* to be hurting him.

"Let's go home."

She looked down at him from the upper step, her blue eyes soft and caring. "But what about the answers you were looking for?"

Albert smiled. "Fuck it."

Brandy returned the smile. "Yeah. Fuck it."

As they climbed, Albert thought about the room they turned away from, that mysterious lair of terror. What fantastic things could lie beyond such a border? Treasure? Maybe, but he doubted it. Besides, more important to him than treasure was *discovery*; the discovery of a secret truth that he felt must lie waiting to be found. The truth of the box alone was worth the adventure. Why? Who? He yearned to know these things, but not at any cost. Not at the cost of Brandy Rudman. Not at the cost of his own sanity. He stared at her naked bottom as they climbed, studied the rhythmic pumping of her buttocks and thighs, and could not help but sigh at the thought of returning this beauty to the surface, where he would have to share her with the rest of the world.

Naturally the trip up the steps was much slower than the trip down, and a deep silence fell between them as they climbed.

It was Brandy who broke this thoughtful silence with a question that surprised Albert: "Are you mad at me?"

"No. Of course not."

"You were quiet."

"Just thinking."

"About what?"

"This place. And the box."

"I'm sorry."

"Why are you sorry?"

"You want to keep going."

"Only part of me."

Brandy was silent for a moment, thinking. Albert could hear her labored breathing, could see the small beads of sweat that were forming on her back.

Albert said, "The other part of me is scared as hell."

She looked down at him, smiled, but said nothing. She was pleased that he was scared too. It made her feel better, but still she felt bad for turning back, for leaving this adventure behind. She felt ashamed of her fear, but she wanted badly to go home.

The two of them paused to rest as the top of the staircase finally came into view. They sat down on the stone steps and stared down into the empty darkness below without speaking. Somehow the moment seemed somber, as though they had before been three and had lost their companion into this spiraling abyss.

"My legs hurt," Brandy complained, breaking the

silence for the second time. She rubbed at her sore calf muscles. "So many steps."

Albert put his hand on her thigh and gently rubbed it. His legs hurt, too, but he could go on. In fact, the pain was almost cleansing. It peeled away the fear, little by little.

She gazed at him, her eyes soft and pretty. "You're so good to me down here."

He shrugged, embarrassed. Of course he was nice to her. She deserved to be treated nicely. "It's my fault you're down here."

"No it's not." She gazed back down into the hole, her expression thoughtful. "When we were in that room down there, did you see anything?"

Albert nodded. "Yeah. I did."

"Did you see those statues?"

"Some of them."

"When I saw them, I felt like I knew what I was seeing, like I'd seen it somewhere before, only in real life, not in stone."

"I know."

"What does it mean?"

He shrugged. "Maybe it just means that whoever carved them is damn good. Or maybe there's something a lot deeper to it than we ever expected."

"What do you mean?"

"Maybe those images were real. Somewhere, sometime, maybe thousands or millions of years ago, those things might have actually happened. If so, maybe we still remember. All of us. The way you sometimes remember old movies you forgot you ever watched. Somebody mentions a scene and it's just there, a memory you didn't even know you had, locked away in your brain somewhere for years and years. Maybe this is like that. A forgotten memory, passed down in our blood, generation after generation."

"That's really creepy."

"Yeah."

"If that was true, then what is this place?"

Albert shrugged. "Who knows? Maybe it's the oldest place on earth. Maybe where it all began. The lost resting place of the primordial ooze from which all humanity crawled once upon a time."

"Right here under Briar Hills?"

"Maybe. Or maybe under some farmer's field ten miles from Briar Hills. This place is enormous."

Brandy shivered. "I don't think I want to think about that."

"Or it could all be some kind of complex hallucination, some kind of subliminal projection. Either way, that's a very bad place." That thing by the door came back to him, a tall, twisted shape, a grotesque perversion of nature with awful, diseased flesh and gnarled limbs. The very thought made his stomach lurch with fright.

Brandy shuddered as she remembered the tortured woman who forever struggled for her life in the front of the second chamber. She forced the thought away and stood up.

Albert stood up too, not saying another word. He followed her up the last of the stairs, unable to keep from wondering what lay beyond that terrible fear room.

Chapter 20

Brandy shined the flashlight into the hole she'd marked in the room atop the staircase. It was clear as far as she could see. She turned and held the flashlight out to Albert. "I went first last time," she said.

"Sounds fair." He removed the backpack and shoved it in ahead of him. He then took the flashlight from Brandy's hand and squeezed into the opening. "Stay close, okay?"

"Don't worry about that."

The two of them crawled on their bellies along the narrowest stretch of the passage and then rose to their hands and knees when it was high enough. Albert remembered the view he'd enjoyed of Brandy when they first came through this tunnel and found himself embarrassed to think that he was now showing his to her in the same fashion. He supposed it was fitting. Tit for tat, after all.

"Albert?" Brandy's voice was soft behind him, like the voice of a little girl.

"Yes?"

For a moment she didn't speak, then, as though forcing the words to come, she said the unthinkable: "What if...whoever brought us down here... What if he doesn't want us to leave?"

Albert did not stop. He crawled forward, his kneecaps striking the hard stone beneath him over and over again. He hadn't even considered such a thing. He tried to think of something, tried to come up with some answer, but he couldn't. Finally he said, "I don't know."

"Do you think he can hurt us?"

Probably, was the answer that came to mind. After all, that person—assuming it was a person at all—must have had some reason for wanting them down here. There was a very good chance that their mystery host would not want them going back to Briar Hills and telling everybody what was down here.

"I don't know," he answered after a moment, unable to lie. "But after all this I'm not going down without a fight."

Brandy fell silent and Albert found himself wondering what she was thinking.

Finally, the ceiling rose high enough for them to stand and soon they were walking again. Ahead of them lay the bridge and the maze. Beyond that was the empty room that bothered Albert so much on their way in. And just past that lay the spike pit and then the hate room.

Albert didn't want to think about the hate room. Theoretically, they should be able to pass back through it as easily as they did the first time. However, the same strategy did not work in the fear room. What if Brandy's eyes were adjusting to the surroundings or something? What if it affected her through her poor vision? Would they be safe?

They stepped out of the shrinking passage and onto the bridge. Immediately, they both took a longing look at their hanging undergarments. Neither of them had forgotten that they failed to retrieve any of their clothes.

Even if they did make it back to the service tunnel entrance, they were still stark naked.

Albert pulled his eyes away and continued on. Hopefully, whoever stole their clothes left the rest of them somewhere on the other side of the sex room. He didn't want to think about having to streak across campus. He lived in a dorm, for God's sake. Perhaps at this hour everyone would be asleep, but that didn't change the fact that his keys were still in his jeans pocket. He'd have to wake someone up to let him into the building.

He pushed these thoughts from his head as he hurried across the bridge. There was no need to upset himself just yet. Right now they were still far from civilization. He needed to save his concerns for more important things, like those things below them in the maze.

He stopped suddenly and listened.

"What's wrong?"

He didn't want to say what was wrong. He hoped he was mistaken. He hurried to the side of the bridge and shined his flashlight down onto the maze.

He could still hear something moving around

beneath them, making that strange ticking noise. Farther out, near their clothes, he could hear another one making that strange buzzing-clattering noise that he still couldn't identify.

"What's wrong?" Brandy asked again. The alarm in her voice was clear.

"Nothing," replied Albert. "Just my imagination." But it wasn't his imagination. Yes, there were creatures down there, but not as many as there were before. Not nearly as many. And if they weren't down there, then where were they?

"Albert?"

"Come on." He took her by the wrist and led her on to the next passageway.

"Tell me what's wrong."

"Nothing." He didn't want to alarm her. Perhaps it was nothing. Perhaps some of them simply grew bored of the socks and the briefs and the bra and the panties and curled up to sleep in some crevice somewhere. Perhaps they wandered off to some deeper, more interesting part of the maze. But the very thought of some of those things being out there somewhere made him nervous. Right now, he wanted only to be back above ground, safely away from all these horrors.

The empty room was just as empty as the first time they passed through it. There was nothing there, but Albert still felt that gnawing sensation that he was missing something, perhaps something very important.

He paused before entering the next passage and shined the flashlight up at the high ceiling. Nothing. At least nothing he could see.

"Albert, you're scaring me."

He turned and looked at her. "I'm sorry," he said.

"What is it? Tell me."

He looked up at the ceiling again, still paranoid. "I think I'm just a little spooked by the fear room," he explained at last, and realized that it was probably the truth. "I'm nervous."

She stared at him with those soft blue eyes, piercing him with a gaze that was almost paralyzing.

"I'm sorry," he said again.

"I'm trusting you."

Struck from his thoughts, he stared back at her. "You can," he said after a moment. "I promise."

"Okay." After another moment, she turned and shifted her gaze into the next room. Those ominous spikes seemed to be waiting for her. "How do we get past this?"

Albert turned and looked ahead. She meant, of course, the hate room. "The same way we got through it the first time," he replied. He handed her back the flashlight.

"Do you think we can?"

"We should be able to."

She looked uncertain. "I don't think I can."

"Of course you can. That last room was fear. You were already afraid. That's probably why it got to you." He did not know if this was true or not, but it made a certain sort of sense, and he needed her to think positively. "This is different. This is hate. You aren't capable of hating."

"Yes I am."

"Are you capable of hating *me*?"

She stared at him, her lips trembling with words that would not come. Of course she was not capable of hating him. Not after all they'd been through together. Not after he carried her out of the fear room.

"You can do it."

"But what if I can't? What if something happens?"

"What else can we do?"

Brandy nodded. He was right, of course. There was no other way back. If they couldn't go this way they couldn't. It was as simple as that. All they could do was try. "Okay," she said at last.

She eased out onto the ledge, still keeping her back to the wall as though it were only inches wide. The thought of what would have happened to her if Albert hadn't stopped her from stepping out of the hate room still haunted her thoughts and she felt as though just being near these spikes was tempting death.

When she reached the doorway to the hate room, she stopped and removed her glasses. Once they were tucked safely into her purse, she took Albert's hand and led him inside. The same gray shapes greeted her and for a moment she felt as though she were back in the fear room, surrounded by terrors that pretended to be memories.

Immediately, she became certain that she was going

to get turned around and walk right back into that horrible pit. She could almost feel those deadly spikes sliding through her tender body. But as she ventured deeper into the shadows, she discovered that Albert was right. This room was not nearly as frightening as the fear room. The shapes she saw were not familiar. They did not seem to mean anything.

She found this curious. Why should the sex room and the fear room have such profound effects on them while the hate room seemed to have no effect at all? If the fear room was capable of getting past her poor vision, why wasn't this one? Perhaps Albert was right. Perhaps she was simply incapable of hating.

She sure hadn't been incapable of fucking Albert, though.

She weaved through the statues, using these thoughts as a distraction. "How are you doing?" she asked.

"I'm okay," replied Albert. "You?"

"I'm fine. I don't get it."

"I don't either. I guess fear is just more natural than hate."

"And lust," she reminded him.

"Yeah. I guess."

The doorway materialized out of the gloom and Brandy felt an overwhelming sense of relief. She'd made it through. She stepped into the doorway and stopped. She could see the shape of the man's mouth, the rows of teeth above and below, and she could feel the coarse texture of the tongue beneath her bare feet, but she dared not make any assumptions. For all she knew there could be two openings like this in the room. She did not want to find another pit of spikes.

With her glasses on, she was able to verify that she'd been correct. The angry sentinels stood waiting for them, the nearest pair about to collide just in front of her. "We're out," she reported. "Watch your step."

"Great job."

"Thank you. You were right."

"I'm glad. Come on."

They hurried on, past the many statues to the next passage. Albert felt an odd sort of disorientation as he watched the statues run backward to their posts against the walls and relax once more into their stiff sentinel positions. It was like watching a roughly drawn cartoon.

They made their way down the passageway to the drop-off they climbed on their way in. Albert paused atop it and gazed down. He'd forgotten about it. What was the purpose of such a design, he wondered. And more than that, what caused those strange scratches in the stone. He'd seen nothing like it anywhere else in this place.

"What's wrong?"

Albert shook his head. "Just wondering about this."

"I really hate it when you wonder about things."

"Me too." He dropped down off the ledge and then turned and helped Brandy down. There was no sense thinking too hard about it. This was their only way out.

They hurried through the tunnel to the round room and from there Brandy headed straight for the tunnel from which they'd originally come. She had taken several steps down it when she realized suddenly that she was alone.

Albert had stopped and was standing on the other side of the statue. He was gazing into the darkness of one of the other passages.

"Albert?"

"Shh..." He was standing with one ear cocked,

listening. "You hear that?"

Brandy listened, her heart pounding with fright. At first she heard nothing but her own rapid pulse, then it touched her ears, a small tapping sound, like somebody walking in high heels, except it was too close together to be clicking heels. It was almost a scuttering.

Albert stepped closer to the corridor, trying to see the source of the noise, but the darkness was too thick.

"Albert, come back." As she said this, she stepped closer to him and shined her light toward the passage into which he was trying to see. With this light, something appeared.

It was just ahead of him, lying on the floor. He stepped cautiously toward it and picked it up as a thousand alarms began to go off in his brain, a few at first, slowly, but picking up speed until his whole world was one huge air raid siren.

It was a small piece of torn and tattered white cotton. It was a piece of a sock.

The image that went through Albert's mind was of their underwear and socks strung up in the maze below the stone bridge. One of Brandy's socks had been missing from the assortment, probably fallen to the floor where those noisy creatures were. But if this was Brandy's sock…

Somewhere up ahead, something in the darkness let out a huff of air and the rattling, shuffling, clattering sound they'd heard from that dark maze began to pour from the tunnel, this time louder and closer than ever.

"*Run!*" He turned and fled after Brandy—who needed no encouragement from him—around the statue and through the passage that would lead them home. Behind him, the noisy creature barreled after them.

Brandy reached the wall and grabbed onto the ledge, desperately trying to scramble up it and into the higher tunnel. Albert caught up with her and, grabbing her by the ankles, shoved her upwards and over the ledge. In the same motion, he grabbed the ledge and swung himself upward with strength and agility he did not know was left in him. Just below him, something large and violent slammed into the wall, narrowly missing his bare foot as he lifted himself out of its path.

A savage sound rose up to them, heard even over that terrible clattering noise, like something simultaneously beating itself against the wall and clawing at the stone.

Albert and Brandy ran, not waiting for it to climb up and continue its pursuit.

They fled down the tunnel to the waiting pool and plunged into the water. The cold was just as intense as the first time. It sucked the breath from their lungs, but they dared not linger. They swam as hard as they could, propelling themselves through the frigid water. The sound of their splashing echoed through the tunnels around them and the waves crashed against the walls in the narrow confines of the passage.

They crossed the pool much more quickly than they did the first time, but still they moved too slowly. They kept looking back over their shoulders, terrified that something dark and deadly was right behind them, snapping at their kicking feet.

Not until they reached the other side did they pause. Gasping, they collapsed onto the floor, and with water dripping from their shivering bodies, they stared back across the pool, searching for any sign of their mysterious pursuer.

"What the fuck was that?" Brandy hissed, her teeth

chattering violently. She held the flashlight as steadily as she could, but still the light danced across the tunnel walls as her hands trembled with adrenaline and the quaking of her shivers. Her eyes were wide with terror, her lips quivering in the cold.

Behind them, there was no sign of the creature. The water tossed and rocked in the wake of their furious swimming. At its edge, the paint can clanked against the stone floor as it rose and fell in the waves.

"I don't know," Albert replied. He was out of breath but not yet ready to quit running. "We should keep going," he said, snatching the paint can from the water. "We don't know if it can swim."

He stuffed the can into his backpack and the two of them continued up the tunnel. He didn't know if it would do them any good or not, but it certainly wasn't going to be of any use floating in that pool. Halfway up the incline, the lid to the can was still resting undisturbed on the floor, but he chose not to take the time to pick it up.

They hurried past the praying statue and retraced their way back through the maze to the back door of the sex room.

Chapter 21

They didn't discuss the sex room as they approached it. Brandy had already removed her glasses and was stuffing them into her purse. She was still afraid of this room, but at the moment the only alternative to going through it was to go back to where that creature was, and even the fear room sounded like a better option than that. She grasped Albert's cold hand and led him through the doorway.

Albert closed his eyes and tried hard not to think of what they'd done in here. Hopefully they could cross this room as easily as they crossed the hate room just a little while ago.

But as the dark shapes began to swim around her,

Brandy began to realize that this room was different from the other two. She could not see the pornography around her, but she *remembered* it. That gray blob over there was a woman on her knees, performing oral sex on a man who looked like he might kill her if she stopped. One of the woman's hands was stuffed between her thighs, touching herself. The very memory of that statue gave her a nervous knot in her stomach. Desire swam up from some dark place deep inside her. She was disgusted to realize that she wanted to put her glasses back on and look at it again.

Nearby was another shape she remembered: A woman on her hands and knees, clawing at the stone beneath her as a man took her from behind. Her expression was agonizing ecstasy. Beyond that, she could still somehow see a woman straddling a man's face, her fingers buried in his hair as she ground her hips against him. It seemed that she must be suffocating him, but he didn't appear to be concerned with escaping. In fact, he appeared to be pulling her closer.

She tried to move between the statues without looking at them, but even from the corners of her eyes, the obscene shapes teased her.

She couldn't escape it. Everywhere she looked, another statue reformed itself from murky shadows into vivid memories. And it was far too easy to picture herself in these women's places, enjoying the same insatiable pleasures. She didn't want to lose herself again to that uncontrollable lust, but she could feel the wanting. It was so hard to resist, especially when it was so easy. All she had to do was turn around and she could have him again...

"Albert..."

"Right here."

"Oh, Albert..."

"What is it?"

"Not working..." She stopped, her knees pressed together against the terrible wanting in her body. She bent forward, breathing rapidly. "I can still see it." Though she was terrified, she found that she *wanted*. She *craved* it. It was like a nicotine addiction, only so much more intense.

"No! Close your eyes!"

"I *did*..." She turned toward him, letting go of his hand, and groped for that part of him that she wanted so much, the part of him that was meant for giving her pleasure. She needed that part of him.

It was already beginning to grow erect—his memories of the room did that much by itself—but her touch was an instant stimulant. The feel of her fingers on his skin was more than he could bear. He wouldn't be able to resist her for long, even without looking at the statues.

Albert wanted to open his eyes. He wanted to see those statues. For the first time in his life, he understood how sex could be an addiction, how some people could fall into such a darkness of sexual wanting. Every muscle in his body was tense with yearning.

He tried to remember the thing in the round room, tried to remind himself that it might still be behind them, slowed, but not stopped. Right now it could be charging down that tunnel after them, but it seemed to matter less and less with each stroke of Brandy's slender fingers.

He wanted to open his eyes so badly. He wanted to see the statues. He wanted to see *Brandy*. He wanted to look at her, to see her in the throes of ecstasy. He grabbed her wrist, but he didn't have the will to actually make her stop what she was doing. God help him, he wanted to let her do it. He wanted to take her right there, and he knew he would not last much longer. If they lost control inside this room, they might never get out. They might just go on and on until their hearts gave out from exhaustion. Inside this room, there would be no regaining control.

That was it!

He opened his eyes, let in the world around him and snatched the flashlight from Brandy's trembling hand. Immediately that hand dropped to her groin, to that part of her that needed so badly. He yanked her wrist from his manhood so hard that she scratched him with her nails, but he hardly noticed the pain through the pleasure. He bolted for the door, dragging her along, and did not stop until they burst from the mouth of the sex room door.

When he was clear of the chamber, he turned and kissed Brandy hard on the mouth, savoring the feel of her lips, the taste of her tongue, attacking her with the full drive of the sex room. She moaned with want and as they dropped to the floor she kissed him again and again, begging him between each one to take her.

They shared sweet, quick intercourse on the cold,

stone floor as the erect sentinels watched with apparent delight. He ran his hands over her body, thrusting with forceful passion that began to quickly melt into a gentler, lovelier thing. Brandy's orgasmic panting also slowed, becoming a softer, smoother sound, less a moan than a purr.

The orgasm was intense, but it was not the same as those they'd experienced inside the sex room. No longer did only the next one matter. Now they both savored just the one and it seemed to last and last as the world around them slowed to a stop. For Albert, this was his first time. The last time was meaningless, but this...this was *perfect*.

After they finished, Albert lay atop her for a moment, listening to her breathing, feeling the rise and the fall of her chest, the warmth of her skin, the hot wetness of her sex, her hair against his face. He could smell her. She was like apples and perfume. At last, he lifted his head and gazed at her, embarrassed.

She was smiling back at him. That was a good sign.

"I'm sorry," he said lamely.

She shook her head. "That was a good idea."

"I thought maybe if I could just make myself wait

until we got out here, we'd be okay. Even if we did it, maybe once would be enough."

"I think if you hadn't taken me here, I'd have gone back in."

Albert was still on top of her, still inside her even. God she was warm down there. "I guess I should get off of you now."

She smiled, but did not speak.

Albert rose and they both gasped a little when he slipped out of her. He then knelt beside her, looking at her. She was lying with her arms and legs spread apart as though she were in the middle of making a snow angel, her breasts flattened against her chest, her soft eyes gazing back at him. She was so beautiful.

"I'm sorry," he said again, not sure what else to say, and picked up the flashlight he'd dropped when he gave in to the lust.

"Don't be. It wasn't your fault. It was that room. We can't expect not to want each other like that."

Albert felt relief that she was not angry with him this time, but at the same time his heart was torn in half. She was taking it all as a result of this place, of this strange underground temple. Whatever happened down here, as terrifying or as wonderful as it may be, was all just illusions from a temple full of faceless sentinels.

Brandy sat up and dug her glasses out of her purse. She was visibly calmer somehow, despite their near run in with the thing in the round room and the terrors they'd faced all through the night.

Albert also felt better, but only in some ways. Now he felt like his whole world was bending into an orbit around Brandy Rudman and he was terrified of what may lie ahead for him. What they just did had merely intensified a feeling he'd been trying very hard to suppress, a feeling that admittedly began even before they set foot in the first tunnel. "I guess we should keep moving," he said, trying not to think about the loneliness of the life he'd left behind at midnight, the same life to which he would soon be returning. Would they go back to being nothing more than lab partners again? "I guess that thing didn't follow us or we wouldn't have gotten this far, but we don't know that for sure."

Brandy nodded. She stood up and took his hand. Together they walked out of the room. It seemed fitting to them both, after what they'd just done, that the sentinels along the walls were slowly wilting, their excitement dying away.

Ahead of them lay the first room of this strange, underground labyrinth. Beyond that awaited the tunnels that would lead them back up to the city.

Chapter 22

Somehow the tunnel leading back to Briar Hills was more frightening than those they were leaving behind. Behind them was the thief who stole their clothes and a vast labyrinth that was home to a pack of ferocious creatures they had no way of even imagining. Yet those tunnels were smooth and clean, of polished stone, like a well-kept palace. In contrast, these walls were of raw earth and rocks, less like a temple than a catacomb. Albert could almost imagine the walls falling away around them and revealing chamber after chamber of human remains, some of them still glistening with rot.

"Do you think that thing could still be following us?" asked Brandy as Albert paused to examine the first fork in the tunnel.

"I don't know," he replied. "I don't think so. I haven't heard anything out of it since we went in the water. It seems like it would've caught up by now. Maybe we lost it in the water. Maybe it can't swim."

"Maybe. What do you think it was?"

Albert shook his head. "I can't even imagine." As far as he could see in all three directions, the tunnels were empty, so he continued on, leading the way.

"Are there any animals that could make that noise, do you think? Anything known?"

"I don't know. *I* sure as hell couldn't recognize it."

"It sounded sort of like a rattlesnake, didn't it? A little bit? Do you think it could be a new species? Something nobody's ever seen before?"

Albert shook his head. *Somebody might have seen them*, he thought but didn't say. He remembered the bones they'd seen as they approached the room with the dying statues and wondered again if they could have been human. Even if they weren't, even if they were the bones of something native to those dark passages, what he experienced in that tunnel was enough to tell him that they weren't just a bunch of overly friendly collies. That thing tried to take his leg off. If he'd been just a little slower getting over that wall…

He couldn't think about that. Not now. Not when there was still so far to go. They reached the place where the newer tunnel was built through this far older one and he paused to peer both ways. He still expected something to jump out at them from the darkness, some dangerous figure unwilling to let them leave these tunnels with what they saw. When nothing stirred in the shadows, he stuffed the backpack into the narrow passage and then climbed in behind it.

When they crawled out of the next tunnel and stood up, Brandy suddenly said, "I feel like we're not done."

Albert looked back at her, curious. "What?"

"We're not done. We didn't finish." She was staring down at the floor, her brow furrowed as though she were trying hard to understand her own thoughts. "We were given that box. We were brought together. We were brought down here. But we didn't finish. We only got so far and we stopped." She looked up at him. "I feel like it's very important that we didn't finish."

Albert stared at her for a moment. She was right. He could feel it too. There was something in the back of his mind. There was the curiosity, of course, the wondering of what could possibly be beyond that fear room, but that was not all. It was like she just said: It felt very important that they didn't finish. It felt to him almost as though they'd set out to disarm a bomb but left before cutting the last wire.

They walked on without speaking, their thoughts dwelling on this odd feeling. But as the next passage came into sight, they remembered what awaited them, and Brandy cursed into the silence.

Albert stared down at the stagnant water, understanding exactly how she felt. He, too, had forgotten about the flooded tunnel they waded through on their way in.

"There's another way right?"

Albert shook his head. "I don't think so."

She made a noise that was almost a retch.

"It's only water. We've been through worse tonight."

"Yeah, I know."

He was impatient with her the first time they came to

this tunnel, but he felt none of that now. He simply didn't have it in him to be irritated with her. Besides, he understood. The first time might have warranted those feelings, when they were both wearing shoes. This time, however, they were both naked. Wading barefoot into that sludge, rainwater or not, made his skin crawl just to think about.

"We don't have any choice."

"I know."

"You going to be okay?"

She looked up at him, her eyes soft and kind. He was so nice to her. She felt almost ashamed of herself to be complaining about such a small thing, especially after the fear room.

She steeled herself, determined not to let her courage falter again, and squeezed his hand. "Yeah," she replied. "Let's get it over with."

Together, they stepped off into the cold and stagnant water. The Concrete beneath it was slimy and something that was probably a piece of trash brushed past her right foot. It almost made her scream, but she bit her lip and endured it.

"Almost there," Albert assured her, and when she looked up she saw the green mark she left on the tunnel wall what seemed like an eternity ago.

"Thank god," she sighed.

"You're doing great."

"I'm trying." She looked at him again and drew courage from his presence.

They wasted no time getting out of the water when they finally reached the next tunnel. The sliminess they each felt on the submerged floor of that tunnel seemed to have climbed up their legs and backs all the way to their brains.

"That was awful," hissed Brandy.

Albert agreed. They both took a moment to wipe their feet on the dry concrete, trying to rid themselves of that sliminess.

From there, they followed the green marks back the way they came.

For a long time, neither of them spoke. Brandy found herself staring at Albert and remembering the fear room.

She never said anything to him as he was carrying her away from that terrible place and she did not intend to say anything, at least not yet. But she knew what he did for her. She knew what he risked to save her. She saw it in his face. She saw the look in his eyes, the blank, distant expression, the twitchy sort of panic that washed over them. She saw the way his lips quivered, the way his skin was flushed of color.

She lost control in there, just as they'd both lost control in the sex room. She lost control and she lost her ability to lead them. It was because of this, because she became so frightened, because she could not go on with her poor eyes, that he was forced to use his instead. He opened his eyes to find the door so that he could carry her to safety.

She stopped suspecting him of any evil at that moment, while staring up into his terrified face as he carried her in his arms like some fairy tale hero, holding her, protecting her, even though he could hardly find the courage to protect himself.

Albert caught her looking at him and asked what was on her mind.

"Nothing," she replied. Somehow, it just didn't seem right to try and explain it to him. Not now, anyway.

He studied her expression for a moment, trying to read her, but soon gave up. He turned his attention back to the tunnel walls. His biggest concern was that they might have forgotten to mark a passage somewhere. After all they'd been through, he didn't want to wind up getting lost now, but luck was currently with them. Soon they found the rusty ladder that would take them back up into the service tunnels below the campus.

Neither of them ever imagined that they would be so happy to see streetlights from the dark side of a sewer grate, but there it was, as wonderful and as welcome as a lighthouse beacon to a fogged-in vessel.

They were almost out now. At the end of this tunnel lay the last. From there, one final ladder waited to take them up into the world above.

After turning the final corner and taking a few hurried steps, they both stopped and stared. There, lying in a neat pile at the foot of the ladder, were their clothes.

They should have been thrilled to have them back. After all, without them they would be streaking back to their homes, risking humiliation, indecent exposure charges or both, but shadowing the excitement over having them back was the paranoia and uneasiness of knowing that they were beaten here.

"Albert…"

"I know." He searched the tunnel in both directions, but nothing stirred.

Brandy knelt over the clothes and examined them. Their shirts, pants and shoes were all there. Only the items they'd seen from the bridge were missing, and that certainly did not surprise her.

"Here," she said, handing Albert his jeans and shirt. "It feels like your wallet and keys are still inside."

"That's good." He watched with some sadness as Brandy quickly pulled on her shirt and pants and then began to slip on her shoes. Such wasted beauty.

He put his own clothes on, not really liking the feel of being without his underwear. Also, their shoes were still damp from wading that flooded tunnel the first time, but he dared not complain. The ladder to the street was within reach, they were no longer naked and they were alive. Now they had only to go home.

Albert stepped up onto the ladder, listened for a moment for voices or footsteps, and then slid the cover noisily open, letting in the welcoming lamplight from above.

"*Albert!*"

He jumped down, alarmed, and spun toward Brandy, but when he saw her wide eyes fixed over his shoulder, he knew he'd looked the wrong way first. He turned around, his heart pounding, and found himself face to face with a man with no eyes.

He stood at least six and a half feet tall, with a thin, nearly lipless mouth, sharp nose and two shallow, fleshy craters where his eyes should have been. He had no hair anywhere on his body, and was as naked as he and Brandy had been a moment before.

Albert backed away, careful to keep himself between this grotesque stranger and Brandy.

The man stepped toward them, sniffing at the air like an animal until he was mere inches from Albert's face. He then paused, seeming almost to stare at him, blind yet somehow seeing.

He took Albert's hand and placed something in it.

"Another day." He spoke these words slowly, enunciating each syllable as if speaking were something he rarely did, his voice hoarse and raw. Then he walked past them and disappeared into the tunnel, apparently heading back to the labyrinth from which they'd just come.

After watching him leave, Albert looked at what the blind man placed in his hand. It was an old leather pouch, about twice as big as the one in which Brandy found the key to the box. It was heavy. He handed the flashlight to Brandy and dumped the contents into his open hand.

"Wow," said Brandy.

In Albert's palm were twenty-three very old gold coins of various origins. Some of them were American, some Spanish, some French, some British, some impossible to identify, minted by hand in ages lost. He picked up one of these older ones and studied it. One side was blank. On the other was a symbol he didn't recognize, two lines twisted curiously together. It could have meant anything. He had no concept of the value of old coins, but they were all valuable, if only for the gold from which they were minted. Yet the blind man gave them to him without hesitation.

Albert put the coins back in their pouch. "Let's get

out of here," he said.

Brandy climbed the ladder first and Albert took the time to give a wondering gaze back they way they'd come.

Chapter 23

Albert walked Brandy to her car. Some clouds were moving in, and the eastern horizon was beginning to glow with the first traces of dawn. They said little as they walked across campus. Both of them were thinking about the eyeless man and the gold coins.

"Do you think that guy was the one who gave you the box?" Brandy asked as they crossed into the lot where her car was parked.

"I don't know. Maybe. Seems logical."

Brandy fished her keys out of her wet purse and unlocked her car door. She slid into the seat and reached over the visor for the pack of cigarettes she kept there. "Thank god," she sighed and punched in the cigarette lighter on the dash. "I need one of these so bad." She opened the pack, took one out and put it in her mouth. She then leaned back while the lighter warmed up.

Albert couldn't see anything through her heavy sweatshirt, but he knew she was not wearing a bra or panties and though he'd had intercourse with her and spent the past several hours looking at her naked, this knowledge still turned him on.

"That was an incredible adventure," she said. The lighter popped out and she paused to light her cigarette.

"Yeah. It was." And it was even more incredible because she had gone with him. Being with her was the best part of it all. He almost wished that the adventure could go on forever, just so he could continue to be with her.

She looked at him through the smoke, her eyes sharp and sexy behind her glasses. "Think we should keep this to ourselves?"

"Definitely."

"Maybe we'll go back sometime," she said. She took the pouch from Albert's hand and opened it, looking at the miniscule treasure within. It was by no means a gangster's hideout, but it was pretty cool. "Maybe learn a little more about that place."

"Yeah. Maybe." But he did not think they would. "I'll do some research on those coins. See if I can find out what they're worth."

She handed him the pouch and then leaned back and stared up at the sky while she smoked. Albert did not like cigarettes, considered them poison, but there was something about the way she smoked that was very sexy. Or perhaps it was only the sex room, the lingering after-effects that made everything she did sexy. Or maybe he was just naturally infatuated with her. It was difficult to tell for sure.

"So," Albert began, feeling nervous. "Think maybe we could go out sometime? See what things are like on this side of the dirt?"

Brandy released a soft, smoky laugh. "Right now, Albert, I don't want to think about life. I just want to go home, take a hot shower and go to bed."

"Oh." Albert dropped his eyes.

Brandy watched his expression darken. "I'll see you in lab tomorrow. Or...today I guess." Their class was at ten, so she had time to grab a few hours of sleep before getting back to reality. But there was no way she was going to make it to her early class.

"Yeah. I'll be there." He forced himself to look at her, forced himself to smile.

She stepped out of the car and kissed him, her arms around his neck, cigarette glowing in the fading shadows of the breaking dawn. Her tongue slipped between his lips and a spark shot through him from his mouth to the very core of his brain. A moment later, when she pulled away, she said, "Ask me again then, okay?"

"Okay." He was stunned, unable to even smile. He thought his heart might explode in his very chest, and he knew by her smile that she could see that in his eyes.

"Goodnight, Albert. Sweet dreams. I'll see you in class."

"Goodnight."

Brandy returned to her car and drove away. Albert watched until she was gone and then walked home, his head spinning, his heart swelling. It had been one hell of a night.

ABOUT THE AUTHOR

Brian Harmon grew up in rural Missouri and now lives in Southern Wisconsin with his wife, Guinevere, and their two children.

For more about Brian Harmon and his work, visit

www.HarmonUniverse.com